CW00551680

DARK PLANET FALLING

DARK PLANET WARRIORS BOOK 2

ANNA CARVEN

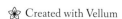 Created with Vellum

CHAPTER ONE

Xal slowly sipped the drink he'd been offered. It was hot and bitter, but its scent was comforting. The liquid slid down his throat, leaving a rich, complex aftertaste on his tongue.

Coffee, the Humans called it. He liked this drink. They would go mad for it on Kythia.

"So if I'm to understand this correctly, you've been persecuted on your home planet and you wish to seek asylum on Earth." The Human seated across from him frowned skeptically, the lines in his face becoming deep creases as he read through something on his holoscreen.

Behind him, a high window revealed the planet Earth, set amongst a backdrop of stars. Bathed in the light of that excruciatingly bright star, the Sun, its blue and green surface glowed, covered with luminous swirls of white.

"That's correct, Prime Ambassador Rahman." Xal set his cup down and turned so he was facing slightly away from the window. The harsh ultraviolet light reflecting off the Earth's surface was blurring his vision a little, aggravating the dull, throbbing headache that started in his temples and radiated to the tips of his horns. "If I go back to Kythia, I will be executed. As signatories to the Universal Planetary Convention, Earth must recognize the right of myself and my subjects to seek refuge."

Rahman raised an eyebrow. "I don't recall the Kordolian Empire ever abiding by the Convention, but you wish to invoke it now, when it suits you? Tell me, Prince Kazharan, why should we allow you and your subjects to enter our planet?"

Xal smiled. He was quietly impressed and at the same time irritated by the nerve of this Human. He resisted the urge to shift in his seat. After hours of negotiations and information collecting and other official Human nonsense, he was getting restless. He clasped his hands together in front of him, trying to ignore the stiff, constricting feel of his traditional Imperial suit.

"You have every right to deny us entry," he said mildly, holding Rahman's dark gaze. "As I understand, our First Division, who assisted your people in the Fortuna Tau incident, are currently on Earth, helping to eliminate the Xargek threat. In the event you refused us entry, we would, of course, have to recall them back to the Fleet Station."

Rahman stiffened, almost imperceptibly. That's when Xal knew he had him.

There was no way the Humans could deal with the Xargek on their own. They didn't have the technology or the manpower. Kordolians were truly their last line of defense against the abominable Xargek. After the Kordolian First Division had fought the terrifying insectoid aliens on the Human mining station called Fortuna Tau, the Xargek had somehow made it to Earth.

Xal wasn't entirely surprised. Xargek were the only life-forms he knew of that could survive in the endless vacuum of space, able to exist without oxygen for long periods of time. They could have simply 'flown' to Earth.

"You must realize by now that we mean your people no harm. The battle cruiser *Silence* is capable of massive destructive power, and yet she's floating in Earth's orbit peacefully, even after being harassed by several of your fighters. If we really wanted to take Earth, we would have just threatened you."

It was Xal's polite way of saying *let us in, or else*. He *was* threatening the Humans, he was just doing it in a civilized manner. Diplomacy was all about implied threats and hidden meanings.

The Ambassador's lips came together in a stern frown, his mouth a brown slash against his white beard. "Of all the planets in the Universe, why did you have to choose Earth? We're about as far from Kythia as one can get, and our planet is small by comparison." On the surface, Rahman appeared calm, but Xal noticed a minute tremor in his right hand.

"Those things aren't necessarily disadvantages." Xal took a deep breath as the throbbing pain in his skull moved to the back of his eyes. "Besides, technological differences aside, Humans and Kordolians are really quite similar."

Rahman's frown deepened, his eyes narrowing in disbelief.

"General Akkadian has even taken a Human woman as his mate." Xal took another sip of his coffee, savoring its unique flavor. "They seem to be quite compatible."

A pained expression crossed the Ambassador's face. "Yes, the woman in question has invoked her rights as as Citizen and requested entry for him on the basis of their relationship. I'll admit, we're still figuring out how to process this one. This, uh, General of yours has quite the reputation."

"That he does." Xal didn't have anything to add to that. Tarak al Akkadian was a baffling individual, and his past was long and complicated. In darker times, he'd played an instrumental role in the Kordolian expansion efforts. One never quite knew what to expect from the General, but so far, he'd been surprisingly co-operative with the Humans, even though they seemed quite frightened of him.

The coffee seemed to be helping his headache a little, but

Xal was growing impatient. They'd spent too long with this diplomatic shit and he longed for fresh air and solid ground beneath his feet. "I'll make things simple for you, Ambassador. There are Xargek on Earth. If your intelligence people have been doing their job, then you know what these monsters are capable of. You need our soldiers to defeat them. I am offering you the option of allowing us to enter your planet peacefully. Will you grant us asylum?"

A wry expression crossed Rahman's features. "You're not really offering us any choice, are you, Prince Kazharan?"

"No, but I am offering you the chance to at least look like you're making a decision. Your people might find the alternative too terrifying. I'd rather we kept relations between our species amicable. You might even discover, in the end, that we're not so bad after all."

Rahman stared at Xal for a while, indecision swirling in his dark eyes. Finally, he sighed. "Very well, I will grant you and your subjects entry under, let's just say, Special Diplomatic provisions, until a more permanent agreement can be reached. We will provide you with residential facilities in the free state of Nova Terra, and all I request in return is that you abide by our laws and continue to assist us with the extermination of the Xargek." The Ambassador paused, considering something. "And of course, you will help us to defend against any other species that might threaten Earth, Kordolian or otherwise." A trace of irony had crept into his voice.

"Thank you, Ambassador Rahman. That all sounds quite sensible." Xal resisted the urge to squint against the sunlight filtering through the window. It was playing havoc with his vision, turning Rahman's features into a brown and white blur.

"I must say," the Ambassador continued. "You're not what I expected of a Kordolian, Prince Kazharan."

Xal stared up at Rahman unflinchingly, letting the sunlight sear his sensitive eyesight. It momentarily blinded him. "No, I'm probably not," he murmured as he stood, trying not to wince. The headache was digging into his temples like a fucking Aikun ice-pick. It took great effort to remain expressionless before the Human ambassador, despite his discomfort. But life in the Palace of Arches had taught him never to show weakness in front of others, even if they were only fragile Humans.

No aggression, no weakness. Remain neutral, but keep them off guard.

He would just have to become the Kordolian the Humans least expected. The darkness that dwelled deep inside him would never see the light of day.

SERA HELD her palm against the bioscanner and sighed in relief as the admission light turned green.

Her old access was still in place. Sometimes it paid to have influential family members, even if they were a pain-in-the-ass.

Dressed in a sleek pantsuit, her long dark hair pulled up into a severe bun, she fit right in as she strode through the cavernous reception hall. The space was closed in on all sides by high glass windows, and it opened out onto a lush forecourt lined with rows of thick, verdant bamboo.

Sera crossed over to the other side, exiting past a shimmering waterfall that cascaded down into a series of stepped pools.

Everything inside the Diplomatic Zone of Nova Terra was manufactured, sterile and perfect. This place gave her the creeps.

She'd prefer the gritty streets of one of the old cities over this flawless, shiny settlement any day of the week. Put her amongst the bright lights of the techno-megalopolis, Tokyo, or the well-preserved twentieth-century architecture of New York, or the charming barangays of Manila and she'd feel at home. In this lifeless place, she felt like an outsider, even though she was dressed like an official.

She was here for a reason, though.

Her sources had informed her that some big fish had landed in the Diplomatic Zone.

Kordolians.

Rumors and speculation had been swirling on the Networks ever since footage of their terrifying warship had surfaced. It was currently orbiting Earth, and no-one knew what the hell the Kordolians wanted.

Sera snorted in disbelief as she boarded the hoverail and took a seat beside an Avein lady who had courteously folded her glossy black wings close to her body.

What the fuck were the Federation thinking, letting these Kordolians in?

The recent Fortuna Tau incident had been all over the news, the unbelievably dramatic footage capturing the moment the station had exploded. The remaining Humans and Kordolians had apparently evacuated on a freighter as the mining station disintegrated in the background. Shortly afterwards, those terrifying insect-monsters called Xargek had been found on Earth, appearing in the deserts of North Africa and terrorizing civilization. So far, only the Kordolians had been able to kill them.

It was all a little too convenient. What the hell were they even doing in this sector, anyway? Most of the Universe thought of Sector Nine as a remote backwater.

Sera jumped off in one of the residential areas, making her way up a leafy green street where several embassies were located. She pulled out her recorder drone and set it to standby, the tiny black device hovering beside her.

As she walked further down the street, she saw that a crowd had formed outside the front of one of the residences.

Bingo.

There were driverless bot-cars parked here and there, displaying the logos of all the major news networks.

They'd obviously gotten word that the Kordolians were in town. Of course, that information came through unofficial channels. Everyone had a source on the inside these days. Mercenary hackers would have swarmed all over this one, selling precious information to the highest bidder. And as usual, everyone wanted to be the first to get live footage of these formidable aliens. The same thing happened every time a new alien race entered Earth.

Aliens were the new celebrities.

Humans had always been, and continued to be, obsessed with anything different.

Sera dodged through the throng, ducking underneath floating drone-cameras and pushing past reporters, human and robot alike, who were jostling for a good shot. She pushed open the glass gate, which was bordered by a neat row of blooming hedges, and stepped across the threshold.

"Hey, lady, are you fuckin' crazy? What do you think you're doing? You got a death wish? They're Kordolians, not politicians. The DZ guards told us to record from a distance."

Ignoring the incredulous shouts, Sera walked up to the front door and touched the bell-panel.

The journalists clamoring at the gate went silent.

No response.

Sera touched the panel again, the faint sound of chimes echoing from inside.

Low, murmuring male voices filtered through the door. She took a deep breath and steeled herself. Maybe the heckler was right and she was crazy for walking up to a house where a bunch of Kordolians were apparently staying, in broad daylight, to ask for an interview.

But as her infuriating father had often said, *fortune favors the bold*.

This could be a huge scoop for their struggling independent media outlet. *BrightBlack* Magazine needed an exclusive story, and what better story could there be than getting first rights with the new kids on the block?

Sera pushed away the fearful, negative thoughts that threatened to spill over. She'd heard things about Kordolians; everyone had. They were ruthless killers. They had plundered alien planets all throughout the galaxies, waging unnecessary war. Their appetite for resources was insatiable. They were cruel, fearsome beings.

But if that was all true, then why hadn't they enslaved Earth yet? Why had they come and taken up residence in a leafy suburb of the Diplomatic Zone like all the other aliens? Sera figured she was safe enough right now, because if the Kordolians had really wanted to harm Humans, they would have already done so.

There were so many things to figure out. Burning with curiosity and trepidation, Sera tapped the bell-panel again, this time repeatedly.

Finally, the doors slid open, and she came face-to-face with the scariest looking individual she had ever seen. From beyond the gate, a hundred cameras clicked and whirred.

"What do you want, Human?" The Kordolian towered over her, his silvery-grey features gleaming in the sunlight. He spoke perfect Universal. "Make that infernal noise again and I will forcefully remove you."

He wore sleek black armor. A pair of black goggle-things concealed his eyes. His appearance was distinctly military; everything about him screamed *warrior*. As he spoke, Sera caught the flash of his fangs.

Holy shit.

He looked brutal and intimidating, and he was every inch the sort of alien she'd been expecting. This guy was like the freaking poster-boy for Kordolians.

Sera forced herself to meet his unnerving gaze. Smiling with a confidence she didn't feel, she held out her hand. "Sera

Aquinas. I'm a reporter for *BrightBlack Magazine*. I would have been happy to send a comm request for a virtua-link meet, but we had no idea how to reach you guys. I'd like to request an interview with your representative."

"No." The Kordolian was already reaching for the door-panel, ignoring her outstretched hand. His body language indicated that he'd already dismissed her.

She must have a death-wish after all, because before she even realized what she was doing, she'd stepped inside. Something about the media frenzy outside bothered her. She didn't want this exchange to be filmed. She had to at least get a few words out of him; something interesting, something exclusive, a piece of footage that would be replayed across all the networks.

"Do not be stupid, Human," the Kordolian growled, and before she could react, one of his hands was around her wrist. His grip was like steel. "Get out." With his other hand, he propelled her back outside. Sera didn't even bother to resist. If he were human, she might have had a chance, but she had sensed from the start that this guy was crazy strong.

It wasn't worth the fight.

As he attempted to close the door a second time, a resonant voice drifted down the hall, speaking an unfamiliar language that she guessed was Kordolian. There was a bit of back-and-forth, and then Big Grumpy released her. He regarded her with a distinct look of displeasure.

Sera's wrist didn't even hurt; there was no bruising. He'd applied just the right amount of pressure. His level of control was chilling.

The big Kordolian turned, shot her a dark glare, and was that a sigh just now? He gestured for her to follow, his jaw set in a hard line. "You are fortunate, Human. Xalikian is naturally curious, and he wishes to speak with you. Come."

Normally, Sera would take offense at being ordered

around like that, but she was so surprised by his about-face that she simply followed along.

It was dark inside the house. From what she could tell, it was a standard diplomatic issue house, like the hundreds of homes she'd visited on Nova Terra as a child, dragged along by her father whenever he'd had some sort of social engagement to attend. In those days, he'd been an Ambassador for the Federation.

The Kordolians had left all the window blinds closed and turned off the lights. Sera squinted as she tried to make out detail amongst the shadows, trying her hardest not to bump into anything.

She followed the intimidating Kordolian warrior into a sitting room of sorts. She could see the outlines of several armchairs and a sofa.

There was something absurdly surreal about it all. This was an ordinary suburban living room in an ordinary suburban house, and there were actually freaking Kordolians staying here. Of course, security was tight here in the Diplomatic Zone, but it all felt bizarrely domestic.

"Come in, Miss Aquinas." The voice that greeted her was deep and melodious, and a little thrill went through her, much to her surprise. She mentally kicked herself. Now wasn't the time to be getting all giddy over these exotic visitors. They were still considered the enemy until proven otherwise. She and the rest of the Human race still had no idea what their true agenda was.

She trusted them as far as she could throw them.

Sera peered into the darkness, trying to identify the owner of the voice.

"I forgot that Humans need light to see." A corner lamp flickered on. "Forgive my lack of consideration."

Sera stifled a gasp as she stepped further into the room. Before her sat a beautiful demon.

That was the first thought that entered her mind. She blinked, taken aback by his otherworldly appearance.

The Kordolian inclined his head, his amber eyes roaming over her. If he wasn't an alien, Sera might have thought he was checking her out, but she dismissed his bold appraisal as simple curiosity. He probably wasn't used to Humans yet.

Sera stared back at him, taking in his elegant features. Long, silvery eyebrows came together in a slight frown. His cheekbones were razor-sharp, gracing slightly hollowed cheeks. His lips were a slightly darker shade of grey than his skin, and they were full and expressive.

The Kordolian's ears were long and pointed, and he had long almost-white hair that was tied back from his face. From his temples rose a pair of curved, black horns. He wore midnight-blue robes that accentuated his luminous skin.

His appearance was impossible, almost ethereal, and there was a wildness about him. He somehow reminded Sera of a wolf.

Damn it. Sera hadn't expected the alien to be so damn attractive. She opened her mouth to speak, trying to regain control of the situation, annoyed that she had been thrown off-balance.

Behind her, scary warrior-guy broke the spell, whipping his hand out and plucking something from the air.

"Hey!" It was her drone-recorder. The tiny device was worth a small fortune. Sera's heart sank as she heard a metallic crushing sound.

The Kordolian opened his silver palm, showing her the object. It was now a mangled mess of components. "No recording," he snapped, and stalked out of the room before she could say a word.

Sera resisted the urge to turn the air all kinds of blue with her swearing.

"He gets a little overprotective sometimes," the polite demon murmured, motioning for her to sit. Sera raised an eyebrow at the understatement, unable to take her eyes off the Kordolian.

He held out a hand. "Xalikian Kazharan. Xal, for short. This is how you Humans greet, isn't it? This 'handshake' thing."

Sera reached out. His hand engulfed hers. It was big and warm, his fingers long and elegant. His grip was firm and spoke of restrained power. She met it with her own strong grip, and something about her response made him smile.

"So, Miss Aquinas—"

"Please, call me Sera."

"Sera." Her name rolled off his tongue, as if he were savoring it. "Perhaps you can explain to me why there are so many Humans crowded around our quarters all of a sudden."

"Does this mean you'll grant me an interview?"

"Interview?" He smiled, revealing his fangs. "I'm not sure what that is. I just wanted to ask you a few questions about Earth, and Humans."

The warmth she'd detected in his eyes earlier had disappeared, replaced with a calculating look.

A flicker of irritation sparked in Sera, and she shook her head. "An interview is where I ask *you* the questions. I'm with the media, just like every other asshole standing outside your front gate. They're all trying to get a piece of you guys. Surely you would have expected this when you set foot on our soil."

"Why should I only speak with you, when there are so many others wanting to hear from me?"

"Because I asked first."

Unexpectedly, he laughed. "Are the others unwilling to come forward?"

"Actually, I think they're scared shitless of you guys."

"We don't bite, Sera," said the silver alien with sharp, pointed fangs.

"How are we supposed to know that? I mean, you guys have been throwing your weight around the Nine Galaxies for a couple of centuries now. We all prayed you'd never, ever set foot on our doorstep, but here you are, in the flesh. So why are you here, Xalikian Kazharan? What does Earth have that you Kordolians can't procure from one of the many planets you've stolen?"

"Females," Xal shrugged. "We would like the chance to meet Human women. You're right about the stealing planets bit, but that's all my mother's doing. I approach things differently. Now it's my turn to ask you a question."

"Hang on just a minute." Sera held up a hand. "You can't just give me some flippant answer and then expect me to start answering all your questions." She blinked. "Females? That's your excuse for being here?" She didn't know whether to laugh hysterically or bang her head against the wall.

He wasn't being serious, was he?

We want your females. It sounded like the plot of some terrible B-grade movie.

Her skepticism must have showed, because Xal almost looked offended. "I don't lie, Sera Aquinas. Is something funny?"

"Not at all." Outwardly, she recovered her composure, hiding the fact that she was flustered. Sera shook her head. This wasn't going the way she'd planned. She couldn't imagine Xal's answers passing for news on the Network.

Nobody would take her seriously.

"My turn." Xal leaned forward, startling her with his speed. He took her hands into his, tracing his thumbs along the callused skin of her palms. Sera tried to pull out of his grasp, but he held onto her. He turned her hands gently, examining her knuckles.

His fingers were warm, but rough. The feel of his skin against hers sent a shiver down her spine. In a good way.

"Why do you have fighter's hands, Sera Aquinas? Is it common for Human females to fight?" He traced the little bump on her left hand; an old, healed fracture. He brushed over the grazes on her knuckles.

"That's none of your business, Kordolian." She pulled her hands out of his grasp, not liking the way his touch made her go a little weak at the knees. He was being inappropriate and overfamiliar. She glared at him in annoyance. "That's your question?"

"I'm curious. I haven't had much experience with your kind, and I want to learn as much as I can about you." He gave her a sly look.

"You mean you want to learn about the Human race," Sera clarified, as heat crept under her collar and the fine hairs on the back of her neck stood on end. This guy was either very smooth, or very naive.

She decided it was the latter.

"Do Earth women really fight?"

"We do whatever the hell we want," Sera snorted. "Military service, systems analysis, underground cage fighting, cross-stitch, you name it. Does that surprise you?"

"You have to understand that where I'm from, females wouldn't dream of such things. They are protected at all costs."

"Huh." Sera couldn't begin to imagine what Kordolian society was like. "Well this is Earth, so you'd better get used to it. Feminism is dead, because gender equality is alive and well."

"Is that so." Xal's golden eyes shimmered in the lamplight. "I'm looking forward to discovering your planet, Sera. Earth is undoubtedly a fascinating place." His low voice was like honey, smooth and mellow. Once again, Sera felt that warm, tingly sensation at the back of her neck. She didn't like it. She didn't like the fact that this strange, mystifying being had slipped under her guard so easily.

Wolf-eyes was getting under her skin.

He wasn't the Kordolian she'd planned for. She'd been expecting some stoic, official type, a diplomat who would rattle off generic, pre-prepared answers. She thought she'd get the usual *colonization isn't so bad after all* propaganda; fodder she could tear apart in a savage opinion piece.

Instead, she got this charming, unsettling, amber-eyed, horned creature, who had completely derailed her.

Who and *what* the fuck was he, anyway?

"What's your exact title, Xal? Are you some kind of emissary?" He wasn't a warrior. He was too smooth; too refined. Oh, he could be dangerous, of that she had no doubt, but he wasn't military. He just didn't give off that vibe, unlike the grim, no-nonsense Kordolian who had opened the door earlier.

Xal looked at her with a deadpan expression. "Imperial Prince of the Kordolian Empire."

Sera froze in disbelief. "What?"

"That's my title," he replied. "I don't rely on it so much these days." There was a trace of irony in his voice. "Aristocracy is overrated, don't you think? You Humans have a much more sensible system of government. You actually choose your leaders." He clasped his hands together, and Sera's palms tingled with the lingering memory of his touch. "We could learn a lot from your people."

A prince, huh? He didn't exactly strike her as the royal sort, yet on the other hand, it made perfect sense.

"So you're the Empire's representative, then. A figurehead coming to Earth to gently introduce us to the idea of Imperial Kordolian rule?"

"Absolutely not." Xal managed to look shocked. "We want to forge an alliance, not become your overlords. I can assure you, I don't represent the Empire. I'm not interested in procurement and expansion. I come here on behalf of the Kordolian race, as an equal."

"As an equal." Sera found that hard to believe. "You want to live side by side with Humans?"

"Why do you find that so far-fetched?"

"You know, we do get news in this corner of the Universe,

Prince. The Kordolian Empire has a reputation for brutality and exploitation."

"I'm different to them, Sera," he said softly. "I have no interest in trying to enslave your people. The same goes for the Kordolians who came with me. Believe it or not, some of us just want to live in peace."

He was overwhelmingly close, and she was at risk of getting lost in his mesmerizing golden gaze.

Part of her wanted to believe him, and that was bad.

She really shouldn't be getting flustered over this Kordolian, but he was unlike anyone she'd ever encountered. He was polite yet arrogant, bluntly honest yet inscrutable, and completely mystifying.

Sera couldn't stop staring at him. Her mouth was dry, her palms were clammy, and she couldn't think straight.

She was reacting to him. That was bad.

As a journalist, Sera had developed a knack for figuring people out. But this alien? He was doing her head in. He wasn't what she'd expected a Kordolian to be like.

The guy who'd answered the door had been what she was expecting. A gruff, no-nonsense warrior type. She could deal with those.

This guy? He was complicated, and that made him dangerous. He was asking her a lot of questions, and she wasn't sure she was doing the Human race a favor with her answers.

Sera needed to terminate the interview, now. She needed to get out of here, because she didn't understand him, and she didn't understand why her heart was suddenly pounding.

She didn't trust him; she didn't trust Kordolians in general, and that would be the theme of her article. If he was going to try and be cryptic with her, then she would use a little journalistic license and fill in the blanks herself.

Served him right for being such an infuriating, sexy Kordolian.

She wouldn't be swayed by his good looks. Just because he

was an alien and a rare species in this corner of the Universe didn't mean he was getting a free pass.

Oh, no. She had to remain objective at all costs.

ABRUPTLY, the female called Sera stood. She moved with an easy grace, rising to her feet in a fluid motion. Her strange high shoes were the only hint of color in her dark outfit.

There was so much Xal didn't understand. Why did she wear such shoes? They had a long spike at the heel, angling her feet upwards so that she walked on her toes. They were silver, with swirls of deep blue. They looked terribly uncomfortable.

Despite their crazy angle, she balanced on them effortlessly, and he stared at her legs, which were encased in dark fabric. The swell of her calves was clearly visible and her pants became taut around her thighs, accentuating their roundness as they curved upwards to meet generous hips.

The black jacket she wore nipped in at her waist and flattered her rounded breasts without revealing too much. She had strong, athletic shoulders and a graceful neck. Her jaw was clenched in irritation, and her dark brown eyes held fire.

Her skin was a light brown color. It was almost golden, a shade he had never seen on any individual before, human or otherwise.

She was so different to his kind; she was completely, utterly Human. Some Kordolians might have found her appearance strange, repulsive even, but Xal appreciated beauty in all its forms.

A single tendril escaped her tightly bound hair. It was curled, something he hadn't even thought possible. Kordolians only ever had straight hair.

Like many of the Human women he'd seen so far, her face was painted, lending a slight sheen to her skin. She had full, expressive lips that were tinted red and her dark eyes were lined with black.

It added to her allure, and yet he wondered why she felt the need to decorate herself in such a way. He was certain she would be equally as beautiful without the face-paint.

Humans. They were still such a mystery to him.

For example, he didn't understand why she'd suddenly become upset.

"I think I have enough information for now," she said tersely. She reached inside her jacket and pulled something out. It was a small chip. "My data chip. My contact details are inside, if you ever change your mind and want to give me a serious interview. You can also easily find me on the Networks, once you figure out how to navigate them. We can always meet over a virtua-link. Actually, that might be better for both of us."

The corners of her crimson lips curled upwards ever so slightly. Was she mocking him? She was poised and utterly confident, and he found that combination rather seductive.

And yet for a moment there, when he'd grasped her hands, she'd been startled, and the mask had dropped. He'd seen a flicker of warmth in her eyes, and a glimmer of vulnerability.

She had fighter's hands, and he didn't know why.

Most Kordolian females would *never* think of doing such a thing. They were sheltered from the harsh realities of the Universe. A cultural difference, perhaps.

Interesting.

He took the chip from her, intentionally allowing his fingers to linger against hers.

She didn't react. That was slightly disappointing, but she *was* Human, after all. Maybe she didn't find his type attractive. He could imagine how startling he might look to Humans, especially with his horns.

When all the other Kordolians in Kythian society went around hornless, Xal refused to have his chopped and sealed.

He didn't see why he had to mutilate what nature had given him.

And he wasn't about to change that for the sake of Humans, even females.

Goddess; this was too much for him to process. He'd come from the harsh environment of Kythia to a planet where he'd seen more females in a single day than he'd encountered in an entire orbit. And Human women completely scrambled his understanding of the opposite gender.

Perhaps his reaction to her was simply a result of having been deprived for too long.

He needed fresh air; he needed to run and feel the wind against his face.

"Sera." He liked her exotic sounding name. He liked the way it rolled off his tongue. "Is there some place on this island where one can run? An open space, free of Humans?"

Suspicion danced in her eyes. "Why do you want to know?"

"I'm the sort who doesn't do well in confined spaces, and I've been stuck on a battle cruiser for the last six cycles. I've been starved of freedom and it's been driving me insane. I just want to get out in the open and stretch my legs."

"Cabin fever, huh?" She sounded oddly sympathetic. Indecision flitted across her face, and she hesitated. After a pause, she sighed. "There's a hundred kilometers of seawall on the Northern side of the island. It's isolated at the best of times. Just be mindful that it's outside the Diplomatic Zone. They won't let you out without a pass."

"I will go as soon as this side of the Earth tips into shadow. Perhaps you would join me," he suggested, surprising himself. Where had that come from? "I would go sooner, but sunlight doesn't agree with my kind."

"Thanks for the invitation, but I have work to do tonight." She shook her head. "I'd suggest you be a good visitor and stick to your side of the fence. If for some reason they actually let you cross over, you'll be shadowed by drones and you'll attract a lot of unwanted attention. Be careful, Prince. I know you Kordolians are big and bad and scary, but you never know what might happen. Not everyone on Earth is tolerant towards aliens." She straightened and turned. "Goodbye, Xal. Thank you for your time." She seemed to be in a hurry to leave all of a sudden.

Xal stared at her blankly, wondering why she thought the Human authorities could keep him from going where he wanted. It was absurd. Even when he'd lived in the Palace of Arches, he'd always found a way to escape. The wild, open plains of the Vaal had always called to him, and eventually he had returned to the Tribes. They had always given him shelter when he needed it most.

It had driven his minders mad and infuriated his mother. She'd blamed his father, saying Ilhan had turned him into a savage.

Sera started to walk away, her scent lingering behind her, teasing Xal with hints of something sweet and forbidden. Earth was full of the sounds and smells of life; things *grew* here, unlike on Kythia, where everything was cold, flat and frozen.

"Sera," he said, and she turned. "On your way out, can you please tell the Humans gathered outside to go away? The General will lose patience soon, and I don't want anyone to get hurt."

"You mean the assho— uh, guy who broke my drone-cam?"

"General Akkadian's mate is unwell. If those Humans keep interrupting her rest, he might get a little annoyed."

"So there *are* female Kordolians." She shot him an accusing glare. Xal blinked.

"The General's mate is Human," he corrected her. "Most females of my species never go off-planet."

"Oh, she's Human? Really?" Sera's mouth went wide, then she slowly closed it, shaking her head. "I'll definitely warn them. But I doubt they'll go away. One thing you'll find out about Earth is that the media are like cockroaches. You'll never, ever get rid of them, even if the apocalypse happens tomorrow."

"I don't know what cockroaches are, Sera Aquinas, but I'd imagine they're some kind of pest. Don't you worry. We Kordolians are very good at getting rid of pests."

"Ha." She smiled then, displaying her perfect, white, teeth. Even though she didn't have fangs, she reminded Xal of a beautiful predator. "You obviously haven't met the paparazzi before. Good luck, and welcome to Planet Earth, Prince Xalikian. I'll see myself out."

And with a final, cryptic look, she was gone.

Xal sighed, running his fingers up and down one of his sensitive horns, trying to distract himself from his raging erection and the dull ache that lingered in his temples.

Shit. Was this how it was going to be every time he encountered a Human woman?

Or was it just her?

He shook his head. How in Kaiin's hells had the General tamed that Abbey of his?

Human females were mystifying creatures, indeed.

Xal couldn't wait until this side of the Earth turned away from the blistering sun, plunging them into the phase Humans called night. He couldn't go out when it was like this; there was too much ultraviolet out there. He longed for the darkness. Perhaps then he could take a long, cold swim in the huge mass of water Humans called the Pacific Ocean.

CHAPTER TWO

As she left Xal behind in the living room, Sera passed back the way she came, fumbling for the wall so she didn't bump into anything.

"Lights on," she commanded, and the space lit up, revealing a sleek white kitchen.

The only problem was that a big black figure was outlined against the glossy whiteness, startling her. It was the hard, scary Kordolian from earlier. Xal had referred to him as 'The General.' He'd been moving silently in the dark, doing something with the beverage-bot on the wall, and she thought she might just creep past, unnoticed.

Too bad her heels were damn loud on the synthetic floor.

He turned and glared at her.

"I was just leaving," she said hastily, holding her hands up in what she hoped was a placating gesture.

"Human." He waved her over imperiously. "Come here."

Sera froze, unsure whether she should just make a break for it. "I'm leaving, I promise."

"You will explain how one operates this device."

It wasn't a request, but an order. Sera considered bolting for the door, but she suspected this Kordolian might be faster than her. He was crazy strong, and the last thing she wanted was to piss him off. She got the feeling he wasn't used to being disobeyed.

She sighed. "What are you after, General?" She made her way across to the kitchen, where the screen of the beverage dispenser was flashing. It was one of the older, cheaper models; it didn't have an assist mode or a voice-command option.

"Tea."

"Okay, but what kind of tea? I mean, you have Ceylon, Kenyan, Rhubarb, Passionfruit, Lady Grey..."

"What would a Human take for an upset stomach?"

"Oh, peppermint tea is good for that sort of thing." Sera scrolled effortlessly through the selections on the panel. The dispenser hummed to life, and seconds later, a boiling mug of steaming, peppermint tea appeared in the chute. "Are you not feeling well?"

"I do not get sick." He snapped, taking the mug without any further explanation. "You may go now."

"Huh." Sera stared after him in disbelief as he disappeared upstairs. "A 'thank-you' wouldn't hurt," she muttered under her breath. She wondered what kind of woman would be insane enough to get involved with a guy like that.

With a sigh, she left the house, making her way back down the garden path. The media throng descended on her as she pushed open the gate.

"Hey, lady, what the hell did you do in there? Will you give us a statement? What are the Kordolians doing here on Earth? Is the start of Invasion Day?"

She waved a particularly irritating micro-drone out of her face and smiled. "Well apparently, they want our females."

Laughter rippled through the media pack. "Come on, give us something to work with. Don't keep all the juicy stuff to yourself."

"I've got nothing for you except a message from the Kordolians. Hmm, let me think. It went something like: get out of here, or that big, threatening guy in the exo-armor will come out and deal with you. I have no idea what he might do to you all, but I get the feeling you might not like it."

Again, there was laughter. "Whatever," a blonde woman chuckled. "You know how much security they've got going on in the DZ. We're perfectly safe here. Although I'd let *him* deal with me any day." She gave Sera a salacious wink before her expression turned serious. "So what are the Kordolians really like? Are they as bad as all the stories make them out to be?"

Sera elbowed her way through the crowd, smiling sweetly. "Why don't you all go knock on the door and find out? They don't exactly bite."

They do have fangs, though.

The smell of rain was in the air as she made her way back across the DZ, itching to write her story. She hadn't exactly gotten the information she'd wanted, but it was enough. They'd all seen her going in and out of that place. Whatever she put to text would be seen as legit.

As she crossed the threshold and entered the Free Zone, the wind started to pick up. Dense black clouds were coming in from the north, towering and angry. It was as if the sky had been split in two; half of it was clear blue, the other half held a menacing tropical storm.

Not that she was worried.

The terraformed island of Nova Terra was right in the middle of the Pacific Ocean. The storms came and went, and people went about their daily business, mostly without concern, because everything was built to withstand a Category 6 hurricane.

Sera stepped onto another hoverail, glad for its cool interior. The heat and humidity were starting to become oppressive. It was only when she sat down that she put her head back and laughed quietly to herself over the stupidity and audacity of what she'd just done.

She'd gotten herself a prime interview and she hadn't been able to get out of there fast enough. The strength of her reaction to the Kordolian Prince had freaked her out. She *never* got like that with guys, ever.

Usually, she was the one calling the shots.

They glided downtown, passing tall glass and steel towers, which reflected the sun and stood out like stark, shimmering crystals against the darkened sky. The twin monoliths of Aquinas Towers winked at her as a flash of light glinted off them. They were an ever-present reminder that despite all her efforts to break free, her family's legacy loomed over her like an inescapable shadow.

The hoverail reached her stop, and Sera alighted, making her way down into the huge, subterranean complex that locals called The Catacombs. The nickname was misleading; the area was a maze of brightly lit shops and eateries that stretched for miles. People even had apartments down here, happy to trade windows and sunlight for convenience.

Sera entered the narrow offices of *BrightBlack*. The small media outlet occupied a dead space between a hotel and a department store; a long snaking space that was only a meter wide in some places. The only good thing about it was that the roof was high, soaring above them and saving the place from becoming a claustrophobic's worst nightmare.

It was a closely guarded secret that *BrightBlack* was Sera's own company, a small startup that she dreamt of turning into a powerful, influential news outlet. Even the manager and the editor didn't know.

Her father, the staff, her family; they all thought she just worked there because of some misguided sense of justice.

She was the antithesis to her family's corporate, politically connected empire.

"Hey, Jonas." She nodded to the intern, who was engaged in a three-way virtualstream with a couple of international freelancers. The kid was wearing a visor, but he turned at the sound of her voice, pointing to the screen on the wall. Footage of her entering the Kordolian house was already appearing on the networks.

She rolled her eyes. They had nothing on her except for that vision. She hadn't given them anything quotable.

Sera kicked off her heels and climbed the thin metal ladder that led to her retreat; a small mezzanine platform that was cantilevered high above the gleaming synthetic floor.

A nest of cushions was scattered haphazardly across the floor, and she collapsed into them, staring up at the concrete ceiling.

Thoughts of a certain silver alien entered her mind. The memory of his burning amber gaze seared her thoughts and spoilt her concentration. Sera sighed.

If he could have that effect on her, then she couldn't even imagine how the rest of Earth would react. They would go crazy for these mysterious beings. The Kordolians were powerful, dark and sexy; they had the potential to become the perfect media darlings.

Still, just because they were alluring, didn't mean they weren't dangerous.

She was going to write her article, and she was going to ask the question loud and clear, putting it out there for all of Humankind to contemplate. There was no way she was letting some sexy, silver-skinned alien prince seduce her just so he could have a free ride into Human society.

These Kordolians hadn't come all the way from the centre of the Universe to distant Earth on a whim.

We want your females. Sera snorted. Did Prince Xalikian think she was an idiot? There was no way she could believe that. They were Kordolians, the brutal, parasitic overlords of half the known universe.

What the hell were they doing here?

There had to be an agenda.

IT WAS LATE when Sera finished her article, and by the time she'd had it digitally edited and changed a few things to her satisfaction, she felt restless. She stretched, loosening her stiff limbs.

She hit 'upload', and her piece was instantly translated into hundreds of Earth languages and of course, into Universal. A digital reader converted it to spoken word, and it was churned out onto the Networks, having been categorized by a few very carefully selected keywords.

Kordolian.

Agenda.

Invasion.

She didn't know what kind of shady backroom deal they'd done to be allowed to come to Earth so easily, but she suspected that a large amount of minerals or credits had exchanged hands somewhere up in Earth's orbit. Even though they didn't agree on just about everything, Sera was her father's daughter, and she was an Aquinas.

She knew how this shit worked.

Corruption was alive and well, despite everything the Federation told them.

Sera shut off her holoscreen and peered over the edge of her platform. The space below had gone to dim-light, and the staff were all gone. From next door, the sound of deep, reverberating bass pounded through the walls. The club in the hotel was just getting started.

She grabbed her bag and used a wipe to strip the make-up from her face. Her scars would show, but she didn't care. She undressed and slipped on a seamless workout top and a pair of running tights. The light Syntech fabric was like a second skin, covering her colorful tattoos yet allowing her skin to breathe.

She pulled on her joggers and slipped out of the office, emerging from The Catacombs into the warm tropical night.

The wind whipped around her as she started to run, passing through the busy streets of downtown. The Free Zones of Nova Terra operated throughout the day and night; it was the city that never slept. Somewhere on Earth or in the Nine Galaxies, someone was doing trades and business deals, and if it was going through Earth, it was going through Nova Terra.

She passed restaurants and cafés, their warm glow spilling out onto the illuminated street, along with the smells of food and freshly roasted coffee. She slipped down past the water-front, where sleek yachts and hybrid landflyers were parked. Aboard many of the ships, their wealthy owners were hosting lavish parties, illuminated by colored strings of lanterns and hovering lights.

As she reached the seawall, she increased her speed, pounding the pavement. She inhaled the salty sea air as the waves crashed against the wall, far below her.

Nova Terra was a Free State that had been constructed in the middle of the Pacific Ocean from dirt and millions of tones of concrete. It rose out of the sea like a grand fortress, buttressed on all side by high walls.

It was hurricane-proof and tsunami-proof.

The wind was becoming stronger, and in the distance, lightning flashed out on the ocean.

There would be a storm tonight.

She gave it an hour before it hit. That would be enough time to make it to the lookout and back.

Increasing her pace, she passed sleek white residential structures along the foreshore, their walls artistically adorned with bio-filters and energy harvesters. Verdant vert-gardens and rooftop orchards added a backdrop of greenery, the plants swaying in the wind.

Sera ran along the seawall, enjoying the roar of the ocean as it beat relentlessly against the foundations of the island-state.

She ran faster and faster, losing herself to the euphoria of physical exertion, her feet beating a steady rhythm.

On this small landmass, where everything was monitored and controlled, this was the only time she could feel free.

She ran until she reached the iconic red tower of the lookout. Its powerful light illuminated the sea below, and as she reached the northernmost tip of the island, she leaned against the railing, looking out to the sea.

The ocean was an undulating grey mass, disappearing into the darkness. Far below the seawall, a crescent-shaped beach stretched out, its pale sand a stark contrast to the dark sea.

The beach was the only remnant of the original island on which Nova Terra's foundations had been built.

She took a moment to catch her breath. Then she turned, gearing up for the return leg.

A tiny part of her was disappointed. She'd been stupidly hoping that she might somehow run into the Kordolian Prince; that he'd defied the odds and made his way out to the Northern seawall for a breath of fresh air. He said he'd come at night. She didn't know why she had this feeling. It was irrational; nothing more than a ridiculous fantasy.

Why the hell would she want to see him, anyway? Especially with her face like this.

Why the hell did her thoughts keep coming back to him?

It didn't matter, anyway. She probably wouldn't have much to do with him from now on. She had gotten what she wanted; first dibs on the Kordolians. Her article was already out there, doing its rounds on the Networks.

She started to run back, keeping an eye on the beach as the wind began to turn cold.

She ran all the way back to her office, ignoring the curious looks she got from bystanders as she slowed her pace, her dark hair dampened with sweat.

She felt energized after her run, high on endorphins, her heart pounding with the afterglow of pushing her body to its limits. She'd flushed away the unsettled feeling she'd had after her meeting with Prince Xal, and she was ready to tackle her next project.

The underground mall was quieter now; the shops were still open, but the foot-traffic was less dense. Sera stole into the office to grab her things. As she climbed up onto her mezzanine, her link bracelet started chiming like crazy. She'd left it on her desk, preferring to strip away all technology before she went on her run. Despite her father's insistence, she'd refused to get a neural implant, horrified at the thought of a permanent device through which a person could be constantly tracked and monitored.

Sighing, she wrapped the link around her wrist and checked her messages.

"Sera, where the hell are you?" Her father appeared, or at least an image of him appeared before her, his cold blue eyes narrowed in a glare. "Contact me when you get this. It's urgent." The hologram flickered and disappeared. Sera tapped her link.

"Get me Senator Aquinas," she commanded, and moments later, she was staring at the man himself, in real-time.

"Sera," her father growled, "what the hell have you been doing? Your story has blown up on the Networks and the Citizen Discontent Index has soared."

"I'm just asking the important questions, that's all." She stared back at his image, knowing he'd be seeing a similar representation of her. "You expect Citizens to believe that bullshit the Federation feeds them? Oh wait, I forgot. You *are* the Federation."

"Preserving the public order is my priority, Sera. I am not going to open the dialogue with accusations of conspiracies and corruption. There haven't been any deals made with the Kordolians as you insinuated. This is a delicate political situation and we can't afford to antagonize them. Unfortunately, that's exactly what you've done."

"What do you mean?" For the first time, Sera noticed dark circles of fatigue underneath her father's eyes. His normally impeccable silver hair was disheveled and the collar of his suit was loose.

"A second Kordolian battle cruiser has appeared, orbiting very close to Earth's atmosphere. They have rejected all communication requests and have shot down three of our fighters. They are clearly hostile."

"How does my article have anything to do with this?"

"You've inflamed anti-alien sentiment amongst the Citizens. It's quite possible the Kordolians are reacting to this. But perhaps that's what they wanted all along. An excuse for conflict."

"That's pretty far-fetched," Sera snapped, returning her father's icy glare. It was always this way when they spoke; they were like bulls locking horns. "What would make you think that an article published through a small-scale media outlet would spark a hostile takeover of Earth? It's obvious they've been planning this for some time."

Her father ran a hand through his hair, shaking his head. He was in his study; she could tell because of the view behind him; a backdrop of millions of glittering lights. "Sera, I know you've worked hard for your independence, and I've respected, if not agreed, with many of the decisions you've made. But you need to listen to me carefully now. At this point in time, the Kordolians are refusing any discussions with us. Prince Kazharan has declined to speak with the Prime Ambassador."

"What?" Sera raised her eyebrows in disbelief. From what she'd seen of the Prince, she didn't think he'd be the sort to make any rash decisions, even if he was a little odd. Had he been toying with her all along?

"The only person the Prince will see at this point in time is you."

"Me?" Sera blinked.

"He's asked for you specifically, daughter of mine. So if he asks you to retract your article and print a full-scale apology, by Jupiter, you will do it. No fighting me on this one, Sera. And whatever you do, do *not* antagonize him. They have the capacity to bomb our planet into dust if they want to. That information, by the way, is classified. It remains strictly between you and me. I will not have you inciting any more panic amongst the Citizens."

Sera rocked back in her chair, trying to digest her father's news. The Kordolians were going hostile, and somehow she was getting blamed? Something didn't add up here. Their reaction was way too extreme. Oh, she and Xal were going to have words, no matter how her father expected her to behave.

"I'll send a car for you in half-an-hour. Be ready." Her father touched his link, about to sign off. "Oh, and Sera? Wear something decent and cover your scars. You're still a representative of our family, no matter what you might think."

XAL STOOD ON THE ROOF, staring up at the night sky. Dark clouds blocked his view of space, but he knew that somewhere out there was another formidable Kordolian battle cruiser. The vision they'd been shown by the humans had revealed that it was bigger than *Silence*, a black blemish on the glittering backdrop of stars.

He had no doubt his mother and the High Council were behind its appearance.

The Empire had come to Earth.

He swore he would fucking kill them if they ruined this world, and he would take particular pleasure in making the Empress suffer.

Cold anger spread through him and he clenched his teeth so hard that his fangs punched through the skin of his inner lip, making him taste his own black blood. The infernal headache that had dogged him all throughout the day and night was still there, throbbing behind his eyes.

How the hell had they gotten to Earth so fast? Tarak was adamant they hadn't been followed as they'd navigated their lengthy route throughout the outer galaxies.

The wind tugged at his robes, whipping his hair free of its tie so that it fluttered wildly about his face. He could taste moisture in the air, and far off in the distance, bolts of electricity rippled from the sky.

Earth's weather was awe-inspiring.

A low rumble reverberated around him and he wondered if it had something to do with the electrical discharge falling from the sky. The sense of savage urgency that swept through Xal mirrored the weather.

They needed to find out what was going on and figure out their next move.

So far, the enemy Kordolians hadn't responded to any of the Human requests to open communication.

He wasn't surprised. Negotiations meant the other party had something to offer. The Empire wouldn't bother about opening a dialogue with Humans. Kordolians would consider a small, defenseless planet like Earth ripe for the taking.

"Xalikian." A low voice interrupted his thoughts, and Xal turned to see Tarak standing behind him. The General moved as silently as always, looming beside him like a large, stalking shadow. Together, they stood on the flat roof of the Human dwelling, staring out at the network of lights below. Beyond the perimeter of their dwelling, armed guards, surveillance drones and combat bots patrolled the area. Xal wondered if they were aware he could see them perfectly well in the darkness.

"How did they appear so quickly? You told me we weren't followed."

"That is correct. I don't know how they came to be here.

They evaded our surveillance. Perhaps they have advanced cloaking. Perhaps they found another wormhole."

"They could blast the surface of this world into ashes."

"Yes. However, I have ordered *Silence* into position. We have three twenty-thousand megakorr fission missiles locked onto them and they know it. If they hit Earth, they die. And as of now, they have no idea where you and I are. I have told the Humans not to engage further until we make contact."

"We can't afford to let them know we're on Earth."

"Correct. We will return to *Silence* and initiate talks from there."

"What kind of ammunition are they packing?"

"The *Ristval V* carries similar arsenal to *Silence*, but it's larger in size, so they probably have more ammunition. In a direct firefight, we would outmatch them in speed. If they didn't have Earth in their sights I would destroy them. I *will* destroy them eventually." Tarak's eyes burned crimson in the dim light.

Xal growled in frustration. "The humans are panicking. They think we're behind this. Apparently, the Kordolian cruiser has shot down Human fighters."

"The Humans will learn whose side we're on with time. And they should have known better than to antagonize a Kordolian warship."

"We have to maintain a record of our true actions, otherwise things will get out of hand. They're already fearful as it is. That's why I've asked for the female called Aquinas to accompany us. She disseminates information to the Humans. She will chronicle our actions, so there will be no mistrust between us and the Humans."

A noncommittal grunt escaped Tarak. The General didn't care what the Humans thought. He had only two priorities in his life. His mate, and his people, in that order. But things would become a lot easier if the Humans could learn to trust them.

It was a stretch, given the reputation Kordolians had forged for themselves, but it was worth a try.

Below them, a small driverless vehicle pulled up to the front of their residence. Xal stared as Sera stepped out and walked up to the gate.

From the sky above, water started to fall.

"Your female is here," the General growled as he stepped back, regarding Xal with a speculative glance. "See if you can get at least one Human to trust you first, before you try and convince the entire population."

CHAPTER THREE

Xal dropped to the ground in front of Sera, his bare feet soundless on the hard, synthetic path. She gasped, putting her fists up in a fighter's stance, shifting her weight so that one foot was behind the other.

He smiled. She was a fighter; why didn't she want to admit it? He loved the idea of a female who wasn't afraid to exert herself; who could defend herself if necessary.

Her body was strong and honed, her muscles well-defined. She was on the defensive, and she was incredibly attractive.

She quickly regained her composure. "Is jumping out in front of people a Kordolian thing, or did you just decide to surprise me?"

"Sorry." He held up a hand. "I didn't mean to startle you."

Droplets of water hit his face and he turned to the sky, astonished by the phenomenon. He opened his mouth and tasted the liquid; it was pure and sweet. "Water falls from the sky here," he marveled, turning to face her.

"It's called rain." Slowly, she lowered her hands. Her voice was steely, her dark eyes full of anger. She'd worn her hair loose this time. It was damp and it cascaded around her face in waves of ringlets. Xal had never seen anything quite like it.

She smelled incredible too; her scent was complex and intoxicating. It reminded him a bit of the imported perfumes used by the court nobles on Kythia, only her scent was pure and clean, instead of being cloying.

It hit him in the face like a cold slap, and he found it mightily refreshing.

The fall of water was becoming heavier, so he ushered her inside. Xal raked his wet hair away from his face, feeling better than he had in a long time.

He peered outside and saw that the rain was now thick and fast, the fat droplets hitting the ground and forming a small stream of water.

"Incredible," he murmured. He tapped the door panel and the entrance slid closed. The cacophony outside disappeared completely.

Sera frowned, crossing her arms in front of her. "You didn't call me here to talk about the weather, Prince Kazharan."

"No, I didn't."

She'd removed the coloring from her face and her skin glistened with a faint sheen of moisture. She was completely transformed from the polished, severe woman he'd met earlier. Her features appeared softer; gone were the dark accents around her eyes and the red emphasizing her lips. Her golden skin was dewy and smooth, with a faint smattering of spots across her cheeks. On the left side of her face, two long, jagged lines ran from the corner of her eyebrow to her jawline.

They were scars; old, well healed scars. She must have concealed them with makeup earlier.

Sera had changed her clothes. She wore a simple, unadorned grey top and loose grey pants over flat shoes. This time, she'd dressed for comfort and ease of movement. The top was quite fitted, clinging to her breasts and her contoured stomach.

Xal inhaled her scent and kept his expression neutral, trying very hard to hide the fact that his cock had gone hard.

He clenched his fists as he breathed in her essence, overcome with the sudden urge to press her against the wall, tear her clothes off and taste every inch of her.

His headache was making his horns throb with pain; it was becoming quite excruciating. Tiny black spots danced across his vision, and the cold anger that had filled him before had transformed into something raw and primal; a savage, burning lust.

He needed to get his shit together, or he was going to lose control.

He needed this woman on his side. She would be his link to the humans, a voice they could trust.

"Come inside," he growled, turning away from her so that she wouldn't see the hunger in his eyes. It was as the General said; he had to make her trust him, and that meant she couldn't know about his state of mind.

And under no circumstances could she find out about his past.

She followed him as he led her inside. He could feel her dark gaze burning into him as they walked.

Xal tried to distract himself by thinking of the various ways he would like to kill the Kordolians who threatened Earth, especially his mother. They deserved everything that he and General Tarak were about to throw at them. He needed to make the Humans feel safe and he needed to secure safe passage for his people; those who wished to leave Kythia in search of a new life. Only Kordolians who agreed to renounce the ways of the Empire would be allowed to cross over.

The old Empire had to die. It *was* dying. His mother and the Court just hadn't accepted it yet. They thought they could become immortal.

How many millions of lives across the universe had been cut short because of their grandiose delusions?

The Kordolian race would survive, but it would be forever changed, their genes mixing with those of Humans.

It wasn't necessarily a bad thing. He wished for his children to be able to look into the sun without becoming momentarily blinded.

They passed into the eating area, where the General and his Human mate, Abbey, sat together. Abbey was reverently cradling a bowl of food, and a rich, salty aroma filled the space. Tarak chewed on a standard-issue bar of protein mix.

"I have missed this so much," Abbey murmured. The General was looking at her with an expression Xal had rarely seen. His hard features had softened, and he looked almost affectionate.

Wonders would never cease.

"Oh, hey." Abbey stood to greet them. She was a little paler than usual, and Xal noticed dark circles under her eyes. The General had mentioned she was unwell, but her green-brown eyes held their usual warmth and energy. "Xal, aren't you going to introduce us?"

Sera ignored him and stepped forward, regarding Abbey and the General with wide eyes, her curious gaze flicking back and forth between them. "Sera Aquinas." She held out a hand. Abbey took it, carrying out that strange Human gesture; the handshake. Xal watched the two Human females in fascination. Although they were both smiling, they eyed each other warily.

Abbey's smile widened, but her gaze was calculating. "Nice to meet you. I'm Abbey Kendricks. You're an Aquinas, huh? As in *the* Aquinas family?"

"Unfortunately, yes. Please don't hold it against me." Sera grinned.

Something seemed to change then. Abbey's demeanor transformed completely, her smile turning warm. She winked at Sera. "Don't worry about that. I don't believe in holding the sins of someone's family against them." Although she spoke to Sera, at that moment she was looking at Xal.

He was sure it was more than co-incidence. What had Tarak told her about him?

"By the way, do you guys want some ramen? This kitchen bot has a pretty authentic recipe. It's amazing. I wish Tarak would believe me, but he's stuck on his protein bars." She made a face.

"Most Human food is unpalatable to us," the General growled. "Kordolians are meat eaters."

Sera and Abbey exchanged another meaningful look, which was followed by a knowing smile.

It was as if they had suddenly discovered some hidden form of communication. As far as Xal knew, Humans didn't possess any telepathic abilities, so what secret understanding had these females suddenly shared?

And why did he suddenly wish Sera's warm smile was directed at him?

Humans were completely, utterly mystifying. In a rare moment of dry humor, Tarak had once told him that Abbey was the single most complicated being he had encountered.

That was saying a lot. The General had been to almost every corner of the Nine Galaxies and had dealt with all kinds of aliens, from Veronians to Ordoon.

"Thanks for the offer, Abbey," Sera replied, "but I do believe Prince Kazharan has something to discuss with me. Apparently, it involves the future fate of Earth, so I'll take you up on the ramen another time. It definitely smells delicious."

Her gaze shifted to Xal, and the glare she shot him was ice-cold. Something seemed to be angering her.

Abbey raised her eyebrows.

Tarak said nothing, his expression unreadable.

Xal briefly closed his eyes, longing for the dark, icy waste-lands of the Vaal. He'd rather fight a vicious *Szkazajik* to the death than deal with this perplexing female right now. Blood-lust simmered in his veins, just beneath the surface, and he yearned for the thrill of the hunt. He wondered idly if Earth had any creatures worth hunting.

He shook the thought. There would be time to explore this planet later. Right now, an enemy Kordolian cruiser had appeared in Earth's atmosphere, the Humans were terrified and suspicious, and he needed Sera's skills to convince them otherwise.

He needed her to trust him.

Her scent was driving him crazy.

Control yourself.

Now, more than ever, he needed to keep his calm.

He would bury his pent-up anger under a pleasant facade, hiding the dark, seething torrent of emotion that at times made him terrified he would succumb to madness, just like his parents.

All he could do was save the madness for his enemies, and pray that it never took hold.

XAL LED her into the sitting room, activating the lights for her benefit. She had now learnt that Kordolians couldn't tolerate sunlight, but they saw perfectly well in the darkness.

What other peculiarities was this Prince hiding? And why had he lied to her?

She seated herself opposite him and he stared at her, his golden eyes roaming over her face, taking in every inch of her.

He had to stop doing that. The intensity of his gaze was like molten lava, but his usually expressive face could have been carved from stone. The look he gave her was both terrifying and thrilling. It was almost as if he hungered for her.

Don't be ridiculous, Sera.

Her stubborn heart beat faster. Her breath caught.

Irritation flared in her. He shouldn't be making her feel this way.

"I read your article," he said, his voice low and soft.

Sera steeled herself. "Your reaction wasn't what I was expecting."

"Reaction?" He raised one silvery eyebrow. "As far as I'm aware, my reaction hasn't been communicated to anyone, let alone you."

"Then why is there now a second Kordolian warship in our skies? And why are they behaving in a hostile manner?"

"That is for both of us to find out."

"What do you mean?"

Xal stood and walked over to the window, clasping his hands behind his back. Rain beat against the glass, distorting reflected light to make an abstract picture. His broad shoulders were stiff, and his slightly wet hair curled around them. His curved, black horns gave him an otherworldly appearance. Sera wondered idly why he had them, and the General didn't.

Were they some kind of symbol of royalty?

"Our history, like that of any world, is dark and compli-cated. It's colored with death and suffering." His voice was a steely monotone. "The Kordolian race isn't united, despite what you might have been led to believe. As much as I love my people, there are those who I would gladly see cast into the deepest of Kaiin's hells." Still, he refused to look at her. "The first warship is called *Silence*, and it belongs to us. The second is an enemy craft. All is not well in the Kordolian Empire, and we are at war with them. We don't know how they have come to be in Earth's space-territory. I have no doubt they would enslave your species if given the opportunity."

Sera's eyes went wide. Things had just gotten complicated. "Are you saying we're doomed, then?"

"No. I will not allow them to threaten your species." The conviction in Xal's voice surprised her.

"Sounds like you need to get your house in order, Kordo-lian." She fought to keep her tone calm and steady. "But what do you need me for? It seems my article really has nothing to do with all this."

"You're here because you are the one asking questions. That's your job, isn't it? To ask questions and seek information and share it with the people of Earth. I want you to be a witness to what happens next. You will shadow me and record my actions, so you Humans can judge for yourselves whether we are truly a threat to you. I'm not interested in placating your people with diplomatic niceties until this issue is resolved. There is too much room for panic and confusion. I'll let the record speak for itself."

"But..." Sera paused, lost for words. This was definitely not what she'd been expecting. He wanted her to go with him into space? Despite all her reservations, the thought sent a tiny, excited shiver down her spine. "Surely it would be more appropriate to have observers from the Federation accompany you." The words felt like sand in her mouth as they came out. She wanted this story; she didn't want to hand it to the Federation's propaganda machine.

"I want someone impartial, someone who takes initiative. That is you, Sera Aquinas. You were the first Human to reach out to us. As a reward, I'm giving you exclusive access to our world. The first to break the news gets all the credit, am I correct?"

Even if it was just an educated guess, he was damn accurate.

"My father doesn't have anything to do with this, does he?" Suspicion clouded her thoughts.

Xal turned, walking over to where she sat. "Why would I care about what your father wants, Sera? I asked for you because you were the only one sensible enough to approach us and request an audience instead of clamoring like an idiot at the gate. That means you're not afraid to think for yourself."

He looked down at her, a swirling storm in his eyes, mirroring the fury of the weather outside. As Sera stared up at him, a flash of lightning lit up the room for a split-second, and he became a dark figure; a creature out of a gothic fairytale.

His amber eyes held savage anger and pain and longing.

Hello, Kordolian. There you are.

Here was the Kordolian she'd been expecting. He was utterly alien; fierce, terrifying and beautiful.

Then the moment passed, and that look was gone.

But it had left a powerful impression on her.

She had to go with him. She needed to find out more about this dark, seductive race, who were not at all what they seemed, or what the stories made them out to be. There were always two sides to a story.

And she had to understand why this male, who had come to her planet seemingly out of nowhere, was looking at her like this. And why did her body respond in kind?

Ever since he'd dropped down beside her in the rain, a delicious warmth had been present, starting in her core, rippling up and down her spine, spreading into her pussy, which throbbed with need.

She had a sudden, overwhelming urge to fuck this beautiful demon, and that was totally absurd. That was why she had tried to run away before.

She had known this was going to happen. The intensity and suddenness of her lustful emotions scared her, and fear did strange things to her. The first time she'd met Xal, she'd tried to be sensible and run away, hoping the attraction would fade away. But twice was one times too many. Sera had a habit of embracing the things that terrified her.

Keep it professional, Sera. For fuck's sake, keep it professional.

"We leave for *Silence* in a half-phase," Xal growled, his voice a low, barely contained rumble. She saw a bulge at the front of his midnight robes. *Oh, shit.* It was the swell of his erection. It seemed the feeling was mutual. "That should be enough time for you to prepare."

Sera's breath caught. Temptation coursed through her. She was aroused. Sweet Jupiter; *he* was aroused.

She could tempt him right now. She had such power over him right now. It would be so easy. No-one would know.

As if reading her thoughts he bent down, taking a deep breath, inhaling her scent, his lips just inches from her ear. "Female, you do *not* want me like this," he whispered, his warm breath tickling the side of her face. Sera froze, resisting the urge to turn her face and look him in the eyes.

Then he was gone, stalking out of the room, leaving her to deal with her sudden, aching need.

What was that just now?

She curled up into a ball, putting her feet up on the sofa, holding onto the warmth and arousal that had spread through her.

She couldn't believe she had been tempted so easily. She'd almost broken one of the rules of her job.

Never fuck the news.

Especially when said news was a big, silver, horned Kordolian Prince.

She knew now that there was no way she was going to miss out on boarding their warship, because this was too big of a story to pass up on. And she was determined to understand what he had meant by that last little statement of his.

You do not want me like this.

Idiot. She had wanted him just fine. Why resist it?

CHAPTER FOUR

Sera snapped a few discreet photos with her link band as they neared the massive Kordolian warship called *Silence*. The trip from Earth's surface to this point had been awkward and convoluted. First, they'd boarded a Federation craft, which had navigated a turbulent route through the storm and out of Earth's atmosphere. Then, they'd docked at an immigration station and boarded a small, black Kordolian transport. Sera had stayed at the back, avoiding eye contact with the Prince, silently observing the Kordolians. The General had piloted the craft. He hadn't spared her a second glance ever since they'd left Earth. There were several other Kordolian soldiers on the ship, and they'd also ignored her.

The General's mate, Abbey, had been left on Earth after much vocal protesting and a terse argument. Sera had been astonished at how the small woman had stood up so fiercely to the General. Abbey had wanted to go with them, despite the potential danger. But in the end, something the General said had made her hesitate. After that, Sera had actually witnessed the terrifying warrior murmur soft apologies to her, promising her he would be back soon.

Wonders would never cease.

Then two armored Kordolian soldiers, members of some sort of Kordolian special forces, had appeared out of nowhere, because General had overbearingly insisted that Abbey needed protection. The small, feisty woman had rolled her eyes but had eventually grudgingly accepted their presence. Their strange exo-suits were similar to what the General wore, and they'd shared a quiet camaraderie that set them apart from the other Kordolian troops.

So that was how Sera had ended up as the only Human aboard this spacecraft. She sat alone as the Kordolians went about their business with a quiet seriousness that was almost scary, and the General and Xal conversed quietly in Kordolian.

As they neared *Silence*, a docking bay started to open. The giant battle cruiser was all sleek lines, designed for speed and stealth. Its body bristled with all kinds of artillery and hundreds of tiny blue lights winked from hits hull.

It was way beyond anything they were capable of constructing on Earth. Humans had only been able to engage in serious commercial-level space travel during the past century, and they rarely went beyond the seventh sector. This thing, if Xal were to be believed, had made it all the way from Kythia, in Sector One, to Earth.

And apparently, they could blow Earth to smithereens if they wanted to.

The enormity of what was happening struck Sera. These guys were here, and if they wanted to stay, they would stay.

Far off in the distance beyond *Silence*, she could make out another looming black shape. It blotted out the stars, floating in space like a dark aberration.

That must be the enemy ship. She shuddered. They were far too close for comfort.

They floated into the dock, the massive black doors closing behind them. Inside it was dark, with only a few blue lights illuminating the area, casting the cavernous space into shadow. The airlock depressurized, and the hatch of their small transport opened. Sera waited until the soldiers and the General had exited.

Xal was the last to leave. For the first time since they had left Earth's atmosphere, he spoke. "Welcome to *Silence*," he murmured, as he came to stand beside her. "After you, Sera."

Oh, so he was back to being polite, was he?

Sera flashed him an annoyed sidelong glance. He returned her look with a smoldering amber stare.

What was that look for? He was confusing the hell out of her. Damn him.

She gathered her bags, which were full of expensive recording equipment, and made her way down the ramp. Surrounding them were various spacecraft, some large, some small, and all made from that light-sucking black metal. The General and his soldiers were disappearing into some other part of the ship, and a line of guards greeted them with a fist-on-chest salute.

She'd left the relaxed seaside atmosphere of Nova Terra and ended up on a Kordolian Imperial warship. As far as she knew, she was the only Human on board.

"So what's my brief, Prince Kazharan?" She put on her best professional face. "How exactly do you want me to 'shadow' you?" If this environment intimidated her, she sure as hell wasn't going to show it. And if Xal wanted her to record everything, then she damn well would record everything, no matter how sensitive that information might be.

"I told you," he growled, falling into step beside her, "you will call me Xal. Formalities aren't necessary."

"I'm here in a purely professional capacity," she replied as they passed the guards. They gave Xal the same salute. "Such overfamiliarity wouldn't be appropriate, especially if we're going to be recording."

Xal shrugged. "It won't stop me from calling you 'Sera'."

Sera rolled her eyes. Stubborn male.

They passed racks and racks of weapons and rooms full of

complicated machinery and devices. Sera couldn't make out the detail too well because the lighting was so dim. Xal stopped in front of one of the rooms, holding up a hand. "Wait here," he whispered, and before she could say anything, he disappeared.

He returned a few minutes later, startling her as he emerged soundlessly from the shadows.

"Here." He handed her a small metallic device. "It goes in your ear. It's a translator. Kordolian to Universal. You'll be needing it."

"Thanks," she murmured, surprised by his sudden thoughtfulness. Or perhaps the Prince was just trying to ensure that she understood everything perfectly because it suited his agenda.

That was more likely.

"We won't waste any time," Xal said, increasing his pace. "We're going straight to the bridge, and we're going to make contact with the enemy ship. Just stay out of vision when you're in the room. I don't want them finding out there's a Human on board."

"Why not?" Sera couldn't fathom how her presence might be significant to these hostile Kordolians.

"As I said before, Humans are of value to our race. We wish to find Human mates. The Empire have a different agenda. They would conduct medical experiments in order to study Human physiology, or they would take Humans as slaves. I can assure you, their methods are not gentle."

Sera suppressed a shudder. She couldn't imagine what a race of technologically and physically superior beings might do to Humankind. "And what makes us so interesting, Prince?"

"Well theoretically, someone like you could have children with someone like me."

Sera almost choked. She glanced up at him, searching for any trace of mischief. Was he having her on? But he seemed dead serious. And he just *had* to phrase it like that, didn't he?

"And why can't you guys just take, uh, partners from your own species?" She felt she already knew the answer, but she had to hear it from him.

"There haven't been any females born on Kythia for an entire generation. No-one knows why." Sadness crept into his voice. "My race is dying, Sera. In one more generation, we'll disappear."

"But you're here now. You would even accept the fact that someday, all Kordolians might be hybrids?"

"The possibility excites me. That our legacy might be passed on; that we won't become extinct. Unlike my mother, I don't buy into the concept of racial purity."

There was something so desperately sad about what he had told her. The Kordolians had colonized and plundered for centuries, and now, they might be gone in the space of a single generation.

The collective Universe might breathe a sigh of relief, but an entire race would be lost.

The corridor ended, opening out into a spacious command center filled with monitors and holoscreens. The technology packed into this wide room was beyond anything Sera could comprehend. Several Kordolian military types were busy operating the equipment. Instead of being symmetrical, the room curved around in an irregular, organic shape. The passage they'd taken must have sloped gently upwards, because they were now on the upper level of the ship.

"The Bridge," Xal murmured, for her benefit. "It's the heart of *Silence*."

Sera felt around in her bag for a recorder drone. Her fingers closed around the small metal device, which was the same model as the one the General had destroyed. "I'm okay to record in here?"

"We have nothing to hide," Xal shrugged. He led her to a seat in a dark corner of the room. "Stay here and watch. And wear your translator. You'll need it."

She took a seat and started preparing her equipment, sinking back into the shadows even though she knew every Kordolian in this room could see her perfectly.

Xal rubbed his temples, a pained expression crossing his face. He closed his eyes for just a few seconds, and in that moment, he looked weary and vulnerable. But then he rose to his full height, staring straight ahead, appearing every inch the regal, formidable Prince.

"Are you ready, Sera?"

He left her in the shadows with her recording devices.

A HUGE HOLOGRAPHIC projection opened up above the bridge. Xal had left her and gone to take his place in a large, throne-like chair at the centre of the bridge. The General sat to one side; a dark, threatening presence.

If these were the good guys, Sera wondered how fucked up the bad guys had to be.

Because of one small decision to knock on a door and ask for an interview, she was on a Kordolian warship, about to observe an exchange that could change the fate of humanity.

Two Kordolians appeared in their vision. One appeared older, and was dressed in some kind of military uniform. His close-cropped hair was black at the temples, graduating to white, and he carried a bit of excess weight about him.

The second was dressed in a way Sera hadn't seen before. He wore bright orange robes and had dozens of piercings in both of his pointed ears. He even wore some kind of makeup, his eyes lined with black, a shading of dark pigment brushed across his cheeks.

For a moment, all the Kordolians just stared at each other, saying nothing. Sera put one of her drone-cams into recording mode, fascinated.

If looks could kill.

Finally, Xal spoke. "General Daegan and Luron Alerak. You're a bit far from home, aren't you?" His voice was as cold as ice. Sera's translator kicked into gear, seamlessly converting Kordolian into Universal.

"Xalikian." The guy in the orange robes, called Alerak, cast his haughty gaze over the Kordolians. He was fiddling with a large jeweled ring on one hand. "I could say the same about you and Akkadian."

"What do you want, Alerak?"

"It's simple, really. You and Akkadian have stolen something very important to the Empire. Our Infinite Mother wants her fleet back." He shifted his gaze to the General. "Where is our Fleet Station, Akkadian?"

The General returned Alerak's haughty glare with one of his own, although his was more like a death-stare. "You are deluded, Alerak. The fleet is mine, and my soldiers will never go back to the Empire. They go where I tell them to."

"You will give up the Fleet Station, or we will turn this useless planet below us into ash."

"Attack Earth and I will destroy you, the High Council and the infernal Empress herself," Akkadian snarled, baring his fangs.

Alerak laughed, an uneven, high-pitched sound. "You wouldn't dare."

"Try me."

Xal held up a hand, as if to calm the General down. "Why are you here, Alerak? You know the General doesn't make idle threats, so state your intentions."

This time, the older guy, Daegan, leaned forward. "Prince Xalikian," he began, striking a more conciliatory tone. "I know the past few revolutions have been difficult for you, and you and your mother have had a significant misunderstanding. Although you acted rashly and assaulted the Infinite Mother, she is willing to overlook past transgressions. Will you not consider dropping old vendettas and returning to Court life? If you forget this nonsense with the Humans and return of your own accord, she is willing to forgive you." He spread his hands wide. "As you can see, we have committed no acts of war upon you."

So this guy was the good cop to Alerak's bad cop.

Xal laughed, a low, desolate sound that sent chills through Sera. "You expect me to believe that after what she did? Do you take me for an idiot, General Daegan? I would suggest that you return to Kythia and tell my mother that she will never have an heir. When she dies, the Imperial throne will remain empty."

"Xalikian," Daegan tried to placate him. "Your mother is not evil. Everything she has done is for the good of our people. She never issued a kill order on you, Prince. That was all lies and rumors, spread by the ordinary folk to turn you against her."

"Killing children is evil, General Daegan, no matter what the end-goal. Do *not* try and justify her actions to me. Ever. I am not returning to Kythia, and you will never find the Fleet Station."

"You dare to defy the Imperium?" Alerak rose, his bright orange robes swirling around him. His jewelry clinked, a soft, metallic sound that accompanied his movements. "You do not understand, Princeling. We are the Supreme Rulers of the Universe, and you are nothing but a brat who has run away from home one too many times. You can flee to the farthest ends of the Nine Galaxies, but we will always find you. I have deigned to travel this far to fetch you because I am merciful, and the Infinite Mother is merciful, and we are giving you a chance to atone for your sins. But still you choose to reject us. In that case, you invite war. I don't care if you have half the Imperial Fleet at your disposal. We will come at you with everything we have, and your precious planet Earth will be caught in the crossfire. Because of your insolence, the Human race will suffer. And the General who dared defy his Empress will suffer, because we will find that Human of his and tear her apart, limb from limb, while he watches."

"Just try it, Alerak." The General stood, his crimson eyes glowing in the dim light. "You think you can win against *me*? You dare touch her and I will personally tear *you* apart and I will take pleasure in torturing you slowly."

Xal was also on his feet. "Leave. Go back to Kythia and I will forget this," he said darkly. "I am giving you both the chance to leave this planet before you invite disaster upon us all."

"What are you going to do, Prince? Fire upon us? We will destroy Earth if you attempt any such thing. We are not afraid to die for the sake of the Empire." Alerak folded his ringed fingers and smiled smugly. "I will give you the duration of one of Earth's rotations to reconsider your position. I would ask you to consider how insignificant you really are in the grand scheme of things. So much so that the Infinite Mother is even willing to allow you to return to your precious savage tribes, if that is what you wish. You can go back to your life on the Vaal and forget this madness."

"Just think about it, Xalikian." Daegan was the last to say something, acting every bit the voice of reason, before the holographic images disappeared.

Well, that went well. Sera was shocked to the core by what she had just witnessed. Earth was about to be thrust into the middle of a war between two groups of murderous aliens, hell-bent on destroying each other. Kordolians were a bunch of vicious, bloodthirsty Imperialists, and the conversation had pointed towards something more sinister in the Empire.

Killing children?

She shuddered.

What kind of environment had Xal grown up in?

That Alerak guy had given her the creeps. His eyes had taken on a fanatical cast and he'd seemed utterly devoted to this person they called the 'Infinite Mother'.

Her psycho radar was going off.

Xal turned, and even from her place at the back of the room, Sera could feel the anger radiating from him. She saw the look on his face and thought about switching off the recording device, but something compelled her to continue.

He met her gaze briefly, his amber eyes holding a maelstrom of emotion, and then he left the room.

Sera decided now wasn't the time to go after him.

Sometimes, men needed to be alone.

The General appeared at her side and Sera turned a little too quickly, startled by his sudden appearance. These guys moved like ghosts. "Now you see what nonsense we have to deal with," he murmured, his expression unreadable. "I will show you to your quarters. The Prince has requested that you be accommodated next to his rooms, and Abbey has requested that we ensure your welfare at all costs. So come." Strangely, the scary warrior from earlier was gone, replaced by a calm Kordolian who was almost civil.

That had to be Abbey's influence.

"Is Prince Kazharan all right? He seemed quite upset."

The General stared at her as if it was the stupidest of questions. "He needs to fight," he shrugged. "Then he will be fine."

CHAPTER FIVE

The training simulator was empty. Xal went through the options and selected a Kordolian opponent, cranking the difficulty up to Level 10. The desire to hurt someone had grown so strong that he'd been afraid to remain in the Bridge any longer.

As he'd left, he'd made eye contact with Sera.

She'd given him the strangest of looks. Her large brown eyes had been full of compassion and understanding and perhaps a trace of fear.

He'd hated seeing his weakness reflected in her gaze.

Xal threw off his robes. He was naked underneath, because that was the best way for a Kordolian to fight, free of any hindrances. It was how the Lost Tribes of the Vaal fought in their ceremonial battles.

His headache was stronger than ever, but somehow his vision had become sharp again, his hearing more acute. He had bitten down on his lip and tasted blood in his mouth, and suddenly he desired to taste the blood of his enemies.

An image of him ripping Luron Alerak's heart from his chest had entered his mind, startling him with its intensity. In darker times, some of the the Lost Tribes, particularly the Aikun, had eaten the hearts of their enemies. On Kythia, Xal had spent a lot of time with the Aikun after he was exiled. They had welcomed him as one of their own. The Aikun were fierce warriors who lived by the Old Ways, never taking more from the land than what they needed.

They had taught him to harness his bloodlust and use it in the midst of the hunt, but this aggression he felt right now was different.

What was wrong with him?

What was this madness that had overtaken him?

Perhaps he was succumbing to the curse of the Kazharan line.

He couldn't afford that. Now, more than ever, his people needed him. Thousands of ordinary Kordolians were starting the long journey from Kythia to Earth, answering his call.

They trusted him. Before he'd fled into exile, he'd been their only advocate before the High Council, playing dangerous politics to improve their circumstances. The Nobles had thought it a cynical ploy for power.

On Kythia, if one didn't belong to a Noble House, one had no rights.

Xal entered the simulation chamber and found himself face-to-face with a slightly imperfect representation of a Kordolian. The fighter-bot used holographic images to change its appearance, depending on the type of opponent that was required.

Without warning, the bot attacked, and Xal responded with a heavy block, pushing it backwards. The bot launched into a flurry of punches and kicks, and Xal defended, slowly gaining the upper hand, his speed increasing as the fight progressed. After a while, he started to understand the fight-pattern of the bot. Even at Level 10, there was only so much it could do before its movements became predictable. He went on the offensive, landing several solid kicks to the bot's chest.

The exertion felt good. His aggression was off the scale. He needed release. Xal smashed his fist into the bot's face and the simulated nose crumpled under his blow. He hooked a foot under his opponent's leg, sending it crashing to the floor. Straddled over the bot, he rained a flurry of punches into its torso and its face, the action becoming mindless as he gave in to his rage. Pain shot through his fists, but still, he kept going. His knuckles were starting to bleed, a spray of black dotting the floor.

He smashed the bot's face beyond all recognition. An alarm started to go off, but he ignored it.

Then, the bot went limp, and the alarm stopped.

Xal looked around in frustration, anger coursing through him. He wasn't finished, and the bot hadn't given him the challenge he'd needed.

"That simulator is difficult and expensive to repair," a low voice growled. "Replacement parts aren't available in this sector." Breathing heavily, Xal whirled as Tarak stepped into the chamber.

"I will go mad if I don't find release," he grunted.

Tarak inclined his head, a look of understanding crossing his face. "Then you will fight me instead of destroying one of our simulator bots."

The General willed his exo-armor to retract, leaving him naked, just like Xal.

Then, so fast he almost became a blur, he moved in and placed a hand on Xal's neck. The movement was chilling; he was letting Xal know he could have killed him at any time. "Anger will cloud your judgement," he warned, as Xal grabbed his wrist and tried to flip him on his back. Tarak resisted, and Xal followed up with a kick to his stomach, sending him back a pace.

The General was a freak; his body had been molded and shaped by years of painful experiments. In all forms of physical combat, Tarak was supreme. Xal's chances of beating him were next to none, but at least Tarak would give him a good fight. That was what he needed right now.

Xal's moves were adapted from the Aikun fighting style. He moved like water, aiming for every part of the General's body. But Tarak had very few openings, and even the ones Xal managed to find were closed with a solid defensive block or a vicious counter-attack.

Tarak moved to Xal's rhythm, allowing him to land blows, matching his pace as he sped up, their fight transforming into a vicious, beautiful dance.

He controlled the pace, challenging Xal, drawing him into moves Xal hadn't thought possible, stretching him to his limits. Where his fighting had lacked structure before, Tarak molded it into a thing of form and grace.

Still, Xal wanted more. He focused his anger onto the General, searching for an opening.

There. The General had blocked a vicious right hook, and was using intricate footwork to avoid Xal's low kicks. He used his left hand to strike at Xal, but at that moment, Xal evaded his reach and connected with Tarak's left cheek, his sharp black fingernails leaving a bleeding gash.

The General grunted in annoyance.

The smell of Kordolian blood filled the chamber, and Xal followed the hit with another blow, his right hand connecting with Tarak's shoulder.

The General growled and closed his fingers around Xal's right wrist. He twisted, but Xal ignored the pain, hooking one foot behind Tarak's leg, using the momentum of his body to flip the General over.

They crashed to the floor, but somehow, Tarak maneuvered in mid-air and they ended up with Tarak on top, one hand around Xal's neck.

The cuts on Tarak's face were already starting to close, thanks to the infected nanites that coursed through his veins.

Xal took a deep breath, the thrill of exertion rippling through him. His thoughts were starting to clear, his rage dropping down a notch.

"You are getting faster," Tarak said approvingly as he jumped to his feet and held out a hand, hauling Xal up. "But work on your form. Anger makes your fighting sloppy. Control it, Xalikian."

Breathing hard, Xal stared at the General. "It's never been this bad before," he said, his voice hoarse. "Usually, I can control it my temper, but lately I've been getting these terrible headaches, and I'm always on edge. If I could go and hunt a fucking *lamperk* or something, it wouldn't be so bad. I fear that six-cycle trip has made a madman out of me."

Tarak looked thoughtful. "Go and see Zyara."

"I'm not sick," Xal snapped.

"See the medic, Xalikian. I suspect there are only two ways to cure what you have."

"How?" Xal shook his head. "I'm not sick," he repeated, suddenly confused. "I feel fine, apart from this anger."

"As I said, two ways. Fighting, or fucking. The latter may or may not be an option for you." He raised a speculative eyebrow. Xal wondered what in Kaiin's hells he was talking about. The General turned and walked out of the simulation chamber. "Get yourself checked. None of us like visiting the medic, but in this case, she may be able to explain things better than I can."

With that, he left the room, leaving Xal to wonder what the hell he was talking about.

Aside from his own mental weakness, there was nothing wrong with him, was there?

AFTER SERA HAD BEEN SHOWN to her quarters, she spent some time going through the footage she'd captured.

The raw film on its own would incite panic on Earth if she transmitted it.

No; it needed some serious editing and interpretation. She needed to analyze what she'd just seen.

The underlying threat was obvious. Earth was about to get caught in the cross-hairs of two warring Kordolian factions, and if the Kordolians decided to battle it out, there was nothing Humans could do.

The only things that stood between them and enslavement were a troubled, volatile Prince and a Kordolian General who had taken a human as his mate.

Xal's anger had grown as the confrontation with the Kordolians went on, to the point where he'd struggled to contain himself.

She hoped he wouldn't do anything rash. She had to make sure he wouldn't do anything rash.

The future of the Human race depended on it.

Sera was finally able to admit to herself that she was attracted to Xalikian Kazharan and she'd decided she wanted to get close to him. The near-instant lust that had overtaken her back on Earth hadn't been a fluke, and it wasn't going to disappear anytime soon.

He was a damn attractive male, and usually, if Sera wanted something, she went after it. But back there on Earth, sensing her arousal, he'd turned her away.

Still, she was curious. She wondered if Kordolians were compatible in *that* way. Well, Abbey and Tarak were together, weren't they?

Were Kordolians good in bed? She suspected she knew the answer to that already.

Sera touched the scars on her face, tracing her fingers over the hardened skin. Did her appearance turn him off? Underneath her long grey sleeves were the marks of her suffering, but the jagged scars that marred the smooth skin of her left arm were mostly hidden by colorful ink.

She'd had the tattoos done to erase signs of her suffering;

the swirling vines and blooming flowers were a symbol of her resilience. However, there were thorns amongst the beauty.

What would he make of her if he saw her naked?

After the accident, her flesh had healed. As a child she'd endured months of stem cell therapy and laser treatment and rehabilitation. There was only so much medical science could repair. The emotional scars had taken longer to heal.

But she had survived childhood, fought her demons and come out the other end stronger and better for it.

Sera hid her scars not because she was ashamed, but because she hated the looks of pity she got from strangers.

Did she dare reveal herself to the Prince, who she sensed had his own demons to battle? Because when she shed her outer layers, questions always came up.

And would he trust her enough to reveal himself to her?

She lay her equipment out on a small desk, moving by feel and touch as much as sight. The dim lighting on this ship didn't do her Human eyesight any favors.

Her stomach growled, and she realized she hadn't had anything to eat since before her run. Did the Kordolians have some kind of mess hall onboard this ship? What *did* they eat anyway? The General had said they were meat-eaters.

Carnivores. That would explain the fangs. At some point during their evolution, they had been natural predators. She shuddered.

They had better have something edible on board, because Sera was starving. What the hell had Abbey eaten when she was stuck on this ship for months?

She slipped out of her quarters, the strange door opening like an unraveling basket, thousands of tiny black fibers separating to allow her to pass.

Apparently, the entrance was keyed to her biological signature.

Kordolians really had the most freaky and fascinating technology.

Sera made her way down the dark hall, activating her link-bracelet so that its powerful light illuminated a path in front of her.

As she rounded a corner, she almost bumped into a Kordolian soldier. He was wearing what seemed to be the standard-issue uniform of their military; a plain, black ensemble with a red insignia on the collar. She wasn't sure how Kordolians aged, but he looked young.

He started babbling at her in Kordolian. Luckily, the translator was still in her ear.

"What are you doing, Human? You are not authorized to be here," he snapped, towering over her. It seemed all Kordolians were tall. "Go back to your quarters immediately."

Sera stepped back, trying to appear non-threatening. "I was just after some food," she said, in Universal. "Don't worry, I'm not going to go snooping around where you don't want me to. Don't you guys have a mess hall or something? I'll go straight there and straight back, I promise."

The soldier stared back at her blankly. Great. So the translator helped her understand Kordolian, but this guy couldn't understand Universal. It was a one-way street. Had he missed out on the mandatory language classes, or did the Kordolians just not care enough to teach their military to communicate with the rest of the Universe?

The soldier must have misinterpreted her reply, because the next thing she knew, he was grabbing her by the shoulders and trying to force her back down the corridor, and he wasn't being gentle at all.

Sera's training kicked in and before she realized it, she'd assumed a fighting stance. "Get your hands off me," she warned. "I'm not a prisoner onboard this ship."

"Do not resist, Human."

"Get your hands off me, Kordolian." It was pointless to argue with him; he didn't understand a word she said. Sera started cursing in English. Part of her was incensed that Xal could just leave her to vegetate in her chambers without any thought for her welfare.

What was she supposed to do? Sit there and wait until they said she could come out?

Being a captive hadn't been part of the deal.

It was too bad Junior here hadn't received the memo.

He was still trying to shove her around, and it was really starting to piss her off. Sera gave in to her frustration and pulled him forward by the arm, dragging it down to distract him while she moved her leg around his. In a single swift movement, she toppled the soldier onto his back.

Oops, she'd just executed a perfect arm-drag and inside-trip. It had been instinctive and automatic.

No-one pushed her around like that.

It had always been one of her favorite moves, especially against bigger opponents. This Kordolian had the size advantage, but she'd had the element of surprise.

"I told you not to fucking touch me," she snarled.

The soldier growled in frustration, his features twisting with a look of injured pride. He moved under her and all of a sudden Sera felt her world toppling. In a flash, he'd reversed their positions, and now he was on top of her, his hard body pressing into hers.

She had skills in jiujitsu and various other martial arts, but she'd forgotten that Kordolians were naturally bigger and stronger.

They had an unfair advantage. They weren't Human, after all.

"You dare, female?" His voice was low and dangerous and his fangs were bared. Sera tried to estimate how fast she could knee him in the balls and run back to her room.

Okay, so in hindsight, it hadn't been a good idea to antagonize a Kordolian soldier, even if he looked like an ordinary trooper. But she wasn't about to let herself get shoved around by *anyone*.

Never again. She'd had a lifetime of people thinking they could push her around. That's why she'd learnt to handle herself. Years of brutal training had given her strength and had grounded her.

In her younger years, she'd given herself to the gritty fury of the Underground League, an illegal cage fighting circuit. As her alter-ego, Sera Rose, she'd had a glorious run.

Sera shifted her weight underneath him, preparing to explode into action. She'd often been underestimated in the cage because of her size and her refusal to get biological enhancements. She'd learnt to use that to her advantage.

The soldier had one hand on her neck, his fingernails digging into her skin. The other was pressed against her right arm, preventing her from moving it. Her left arm, however, was free. Perhaps a thumb to the eye socket would get this ball rolling.

She took a deep breath, centering herself.

But just as she was about to strike, the soldier was lifted off her.

Xal loomed over them with a face like thunder, hauling the soldier up by his collar. "What are you doing?"

"She was trespassing, your Highness." The soldier's voice came out as a hoarse rasp, the stiff collar pulled tight around his neck. "I tried to re-direct her, but she attacked me."

"Oh?" Xal's voice was deceptively soft, his eyes promising pain. "Is that why you were sprawled on top of her like a common *jarlek*? Are you telling me you were unable to contain one defenseless Human female without resorting to brute force?"

Sera snorted, taking offense at that last part. She was *not* defenseless. She got to her feet, straightening her clothes.

"She attacked me," the soldier repeated. "Caught me by surprise. I was not expect—"

"Did you not receive the message, soldier? She is an

honored guest aboard this vessel. You are to assist her, not restrain her like a common criminal."

"My Prince, I was unaware. I apologize, however I was unable to understand her. She does not speak Kordolian."

"And you don't speak Universal? You're a new recruit, aren't you? What is your name, soldier?"

"Erras, your Highness. Malion Erras." He gasped as Xal tightened his collar.

Xal took a deep breath, holding the soldier there for several seconds before releasing him. Erras stumbled and slapped his hand onto the wall, trying to regain his balance. He was breathing heavily.

"You are to report to General Akkadian," Xal commanded. "You will undertake training in Universal and one Human language of your choice. We don't play by the rules of the Old Empire anymore, soldier. I want you to think for yourself, not blindly follow commands. Humans are to be treated as equals, and if I ever hear of you troubling this female again, I will send you to fight Xargek on Earth alongside the First Division." He raised an eyebrow. "Oh, and you will undergo an extra phase of simulator training for the next three cycles. If what you're telling me is true, then your technique needs work."

The soldier regarded Xal with disbelief. Then, it was as if a light went on inside his head as he realized he was getting a reprieve. He banged his fist on his chest in acknowledgement and slunk away down the corridor, his shoulders slumping in relief.

Xal rushed to Sera's side, his eyes full of concern. "Did that idiot hurt you?"

"I'm fine," she shrugged. If he had seen some of the hits she had taken back in her fighting days, he wouldn't be so worried. "I'm sorry. I should have co-operated with that guy and not caused a fuss. I just lost my temper."

"Don't be silly," Xal murmured, his gaze roaming over her face. The terrible anger she had witnessed earlier was gone.

Sera took a step back, regarding Xal with curiosity.

A black bruise was starting to blossom over one cheek, and there was a cut above his eye, caked with dried blood. His wild hair was even more disheveled, and his dark blue robes were loosely belted, hanging around his tall frame as if they'd been hastily thrown on.

"What the hell happened to you?" She was standing against the wall, and he moved closer, trapping her with his mesmerizing eyes.

"Training bruises. I needed to release some pent-up frustration," he replied, looking at her carefully. "Are you sure you aren't hurt? I will send for the medic if you need her."

"Relax, Prince. I'm not made of glass." He was close enough that his scent surrounded her. It reminded her of rain and morning in a pine forest. "And more importantly, are *you* okay?"

She studied his face. He looked like a beautiful demon who'd been in a cage fight.

One of his horns was grazed, the black surface torn away to reveal raw grey tissue underneath. She looked closely and saw that his horns were smooth and covered in a fine black layer, like microscopic velvet. "Look at you," she murmured, reaching out to touch the graze.

At first, he flinched. She moved her fingers along his horn and he let out a slow, shuddering sigh. He closed his eyes and his eyelids fluttered in pleasure, his long, almost-white eyelashes contrasting starkly with his silver-grey skin.

He had such beautiful eyelashes.

"Don't," he whispered, his voice cracking, but Sera ignored him.

"You like that, don't you?" She curled her fingers around his horn, stroking it gently.

"Don't tempt me," he warned, a low tremor in his voice.

"Why not?" Sera was fascinated by his response to her touch. His lips were slightly parted, showing the twin points of his fangs. His arousal was a powerful aphrodisiac; she was becoming wet. She longed to tear off his robes and discover what lay underneath.

"I don't have very good self-control right now." Xal reached out and placed his fingers at her temple, running them through her curly hair. He inhaled deeply, trembling a little.

His touch was like wildfire, sending delicious, tingling warmth right through her. Her pussy throbbed with a need that was almost painful, and she knew then and there that she needed his touch; she needed him inside her.

"I don't have very good self-control either." Sera stared at Xal's sensual, kissable lips. She wanted to taste him.

"I don't want to hurt you." His long fingers caressed the side of her face, trailing over her scars.

Sera laughed softly. "I'm not as fragile as you think, Xal. I've taken a few hits in my time. You won't hurt me."

"Ah." His eyes were still closed, and there was something almost ethereal about him. She found his alienness so seductive; he was wild and forbidden and unlike anyone she had encountered before.

He leaned in, putting his lips against her ear. "Are you sure, female?"

She responded by pulling him down the corridor, in the direction of her quarters. She was about to break her golden rule of journalism, and she didn't care.

Screw the rules.

She wanted this mystifying creature, and she would have him.

CHAPTER SIX

Xal allowed himself to be led, enjoying her assertiveness as she pulled him down the corridor, one hand curled around his, their fingers entwined. He had given up on trying to resist. Instead, he gave in to his lust, allowing himself to be overwhelmed by her.

Her scent was all around him; a delicate, layered perfume on top, and underneath, the undeniably feminine essence of *her*.

He opened his eyes and watched her from behind, his gaze traveling over the rounded curves of her perfect ass. As she walked, her hips swayed and her ass moved up and down, driving him nuts.

After releasing his pent-up aggression fighting the General, he thought he'd be level-headed enough to avoid this kind of situation. But as soon as she'd touched his ultra-sensitive horns, he'd known he was lost.

The lust had never abated, and under the fabric of his loosely belted robes, his cock strained, his erection almost painful.

When he'd seen that soldier on top of her, he'd almost lost it. It had taken every bit of his self-control to do the rational thing. If he hadn't sparred with Tarak in the simulation room, he didn't know what he might have done.

Xal stopped at the entrance to his chambers, which were closer than Sera's, and the Qualum door unfused as it registered his presence. He pulled her inside, drawing her close to him. Her body was warm and soft, and he buried his nose in her hair, luxuriating in the feel of it; inhaling her scent.

He couldn't get enough of her scent.

He looked down into eyes that were dark and filled with desire, her black pupils dilated in the dim light.

A low growl escaped him, and he tucked his fingers under the hem of her pants, pulling them down. They dropped to the floor, and she stepped out of them, slipping off her soft shoes.

She wore a tiny black undergarment that hid her sex and curved over her hips, completely revealing her bottom. Her legs were muscular and toned, and as she stood on her toes, leaning into him, he saw the outline of her well defined calves.

She had a powerful body, which was honed for movement. He began to lift her top, but she stopped him. "You first," she said. "What does a Kordolian male look like, under those robes?"

She untied the loose belt at his waist and slid the garment off his shoulders, allowing it to drop to the floor. There was a sharp intake of breath as she took him in, and then she smiled.

She rested one hand on his bare chest, trailing her fingers down his stomach, curling them around his erection.

Xal groaned with barely restrained need. He wanted to tear off the rest of her clothes and fuck her savagely, but he resisted. It would be better to savor every last, delicious, drawn-out moment.

She took his hand into hers and guided him down to her pussy. He placed his fingers on her soft mound, feeling her wetness through the thin, silken fabric of her undergarment. A low, guttural sound reverberated from his throat. She pressed herself against him, teasing him. He hooked his fingers under the thin band circling her hips and tore the flimsy garment free, tossing it away.

She was wet and she was ready. He wanted to hear her cry out in pleasure under his touch. He wanted her to beg for him.

She had led him to this, and now it was his turn.

"Take off your top," he told her, as he slid one finger between her moist folds. "I want to see all of you."

There was a moment of hesitation, and he saw doubt in her eyes. For the first time since he had met her, she looked vulnerable.

"It's all right," he whispered, lifting the thin garment. She removed it slowly, crossing her arms, revealing the smooth, brown skin of her stomach and her full, round breasts. A black undergarment cradled her breasts, and he looked for a way to unfasten it, tugging at the bonds that held it tight.

She laughed, a low, throaty, intoxicating sound. "Unhooking a bra is a skill you're going to have to learn, big boy. It's a centuries-old Earth mating ritual."

"Then I shall study this technique," Xal purred, as he found the clasp. The garment came loose, and he dropped it, cupping her breasts. He bent down and took one nipple between his lips, circling it with his tongue. It firmed in response to his touch, and Sera moaned, arcing her back.

Xal slid an arm behind her, running his fingers along the lean contours of her back, moving across to taste her other nipple, sucking it slowly.

Her scent was driving him wild. He tasted sweetness and salt on her skin, and he savored its warmth against his tongue. His acute hearing picked up the hammering of her heart, beating a steady rhythm to her arousal. His fangs grazed the soft skin of her breast, and she shivered in anticipation.

Xal rose, cupping her face in his hands, capturing her mouth with his.

She yielded to his intense kisses, her tongue probing curiously, tentatively brushing against his fangs. He released her, running his hands through her curled hair, meeting her gaze.

Her eyes were wide, and a faint, pink hue had spread across her cheeks.

He was still in disbelief that this lovely creature was here before him, his for the taking, and that she wanted him.

He was alien to her; a different species, and yet they were similar enough to be compatible. She was an enticing mystery that he wanted to unravel, even as their worlds balanced on a knife's edge, the slightest mistake tipping them into oblivion.

He wanted to taste her.

He kissed the long lines of scarred flesh that ran from her temple, along her cheek, down to her jawline. They were marks of pain, suffered and overcome, worn proudly. He found them beautiful.

He looked down and saw that her left arm was covered in a riot of color. Exotic flowers bloomed amongst verdant green vines. The artwork was intricately detailed, swirling around the toned curves of her biceps, trailing down her forearm, curling over her shoulder. Underneath, he could see more scars, artfully hidden amongst the flowers and leaves.

He hadn't known that Humans marked themselves in such ways. When he had first encountered her, with her formal suit and made-up face, he wouldn't have been able to tell that she wore such proud marks underneath.

Mesmerized, he traced his fingers down her arm, trailing over roughened scar tissue and the smooth, soft skin in-between.

She'd revealed a secret, hidden part of herself.

He kissed every part of her, right down to her fingers, and up close, he could see that there were thorns depicted amongst the beautiful flowers and vines.

He dropped to his knees, looking up to see that she was delighted with his response, her dark eyes brimming with confidence. She held such power over him in this moment, and she knew it.

It stoked Xal's arousal even further.

It would please him to hear her voice as she climaxed.

He brought his lips against her sex, kissing here there, tenderly at first. Then he slid his tongue between her moist folds, tasting her salty wetness, getting intense satisfaction from the sound of her pleasure as she moaned. Her strong hands curled around his horns and a wonderful tingling sensation spread through his skull, erasing any traces of his excruciating headache.

He went deeper with his tongue, and she bucked against him, gasping. He laughed at the sheer joy and freedom of it. He moved his tongue up and down, finding her incredibly responsive. With just the slightest flick, she would tremble and moan with pleasure.

He searched and found that tender little nub, just where he'd thought it would be. Human anatomy wasn't so different, after all. Xal sucked on that delicate point, and her moans turned into cries, becoming louder as he sucked a little harder. Her hands were all over his horns, moving up and down, her fingers at times sliding down to rake through his long hair.

With his mouth on her clit, he slid one, then two fingers inside her pussy, being careful to retract his sharp nails. She was moist and tight inside and he stretched her a little, causing her to gyrate her hips against him.

"You're impossible," she gasped. "What fucking planet are you from?"

He responded by flicking his tongue against her clit and glancing up at her face. She met his gaze for a brief moment, then closed her eyes and screamed.

———

SERA WAS IN ANOTHER WORLD. She'd looked into

Xal's burning amber eyes for just a few seconds, and she'd seen them crinkle in amusement. The bastard. He was driving her to insane heights and he *knew* it.

She was helpless before him and he was all too aware of it.

He was enjoying her pleasure, and all she could do was close her eyes as sensation overwhelmed her, brought upon by this dark, sinful creature.

His tongue was impossible.

His kiss was impossible.

He was impossible.

She was hopelessly attracted to him; she had been from the start. His body was paradise. When she'd dropped his robes she'd stood in astonished silence, her eyes raking over his honed, muscular torso.

He'd watched her with a molten, possessive gaze, and she'd found herself wanting him with an intensity that terrified her.

She'd never felt this way before about any human, so how could an alien, a being from a distant, dark planet, make her feel so good?

In some remote corner of her mind, the thought occurred to her that she didn't really *know* him, but that thought was washed away by her overwhelming desire.

He was perfect. From his elegant, aristocratic features, to the symmetrical curves of his black horns, to his pointed ears and his silken, moonlight hair, he was magnificent. He was temptation wrapped up in an otherworldly package.

And he had embraced Sera's imperfections without hesitation, taking her as she was.

She grabbed his horns, anchoring herself as he teased her clit, his long, smooth tongue stroking her most sensitive part.

Sera was going to come. She knew it. He knew it. The sensation started at the base of her spine, rippling through her core, and she rocked back and forth, as Xal thrust his fingers deep inside her.

He stopped then, holding her at the edge of climax, and she looked down in disbelief.

He pulled away, watching her, his grey lips glistening with the taste of *her*, and she quivered, desperately wanting release.

His fingers were still inside her.

The corners of his lips turned upwards in a cheeky, knowing smile.

He held her there, just a little longer, as she stared down at his luminous face, held captive to his wild, alien beauty.

Beautiful bastard. He held her there, because he knew he could, and she trembled, because at that very moment, she was helpless.

He raised a questioning eyebrow.

Sera wanted to curse him and fuck him and she felt she would explode if he didn't touch her again.

"Please," she rasped, lapsing back to English, her native tongue.

"I don't understand that language," he rumbled with dark amusement, his voice loaded with unfinished promises.

"Please," she whispered, finding the Universal tongue somewhere in the depths of her scrambled brain.

Just as the sensation stared to fade, he pushed his fingers deeper inside her and put his lips to her pussy. He sucked on her clit, gently at first, his warm, insistent tongue darting back and forth.

Then he went faster and faster, and that feeling was back; that exquisite tightness that built and built until she could take it no more.

It exploded in a torrent of bliss, and she closed her eyes, seeing stars in the blackness.

Sera screamed in pure euphoria and climaxed.

Xal withdrew his hand, withdrew his lips, and brought his arms around her, rising slowly as she shook with the after-shocks of pleasure.

He lifted her with ease, bringing her to his bed. He lay her down gently and moved over her, never once breaking eye contact. His massive erection brushed against her stomach as he lowered himself, burying his nose into the crook of her neck and inhaling her scent.

She wrapped her fingers around his cock, feeling the raised ridges of flesh that ran down the front of its length. Aside from a few spectacular differences, Humans and Kordolians were quite similar, and absolutely compatible.

Sera could no longer argue with that fact.

Xal looked at her with hunger smoldering in his golden eyes. It had been there the whole time, but now that he had her underneath him, he unleashed it, entering her in a single, powerful movement. He went deep, and she gasped. He grabbed her hands and placed them on his horns, curling her fingers around them. He wrapped his hands around her ass, drawing her close to him, and she brought her strong legs around him.

Then he fucked her, at first slow and deep, then faster and harder as she squeezed her legs around him. His arms came down on either side of her, taut with corded muscle, and she hooked her arms around his neck, her fingers slipping down to trace the defined contours of his back.

His movements became more intense, and his heat melted into her, causing her skin to become slick with sweat. Kordolians, on the other hand, didn't seem to sweat.

But he was warm and he was making love to her like the world was about to end.

Maybe it was.

She didn't care anymore.

Time blurred, and she lost herself to the rhythm of their lovemaking, their bodies moving together as one. She allowed him to take over, and he responded with grunts of satisfaction, at times kissing her here and there, nibbling her ear, inhaling her scent. His fangs grazed her skin, but he never, ever broke it, his movements savage but controlled.

He fucked her with a wild intensity that built, bit by bit, until he brought her back to that blissful precipice. He obviously no longer feared that she was some gentle waif, because he slammed his hips into her, and she dug her fingernails into his back, her strong body wrapped around his.

He brought her back to the edge of climax, and he was also there, because a low, rumbling growl issued from his throat, as he plunged deeper inside of her. The growl became a full-throated cry as he went faster, harder, dragging her to the precipice.

They were almost there.

More.

It felt so good. She didn't want it to end, but she needed release. Xal was taking her there. This male was claiming her, making her his, and she was hopelessly lost to him.

Almost.

He took her higher, filling her need completely.

There.

He held her to him, surrounding her with his powerful arms as a tremor coursed through him.

Sera was overwhelmed, drowning in sensation.

Xal was all over her, running his hands through her hair as he drew her face close to his and stared into her eyes, and Sera was lost in swirls of molten amber.

Then, he came, closing his eyes, an expression of bliss crossing his exquisite features.

Sera's voice mingled with his as he cried out in Kordolian, clutching her tightly to him.

He tipped his face towards the heavens and exhaled. They stayed like that for a moment, in suspended disbelief.

Then, in one swift movement, he reversed their positions so she was on top of him, looking down.

His expression was no longer an inscrutable one; his face had softened, and he shook his head slightly in disbelief.

"You are beautiful, Sera Aquinas," he murmured, taking her in with a half-lidded gaze.

"So are you, Xal," she replied. Exhausted, she rested her cheek against his bare chest and closed her eyes, listening to the beat of his Kordolian heart.

Their hearts beat the same.

They breathed the same air.

They fucked the same.

It seemed Humans and Kordolians weren't so different after all.

CHAPTER SEVEN

Sera must have dozed off, because when she came to, he was running his long fingers through her hair.

She made a low sound in her throat as her eyes drooped again. She was warm and cocooned in a sleeping pod on a mysterious alien ship, and she had never felt so contented in her life.

No-one had ever held Sera like this. She'd never woken up with another by her side.

Usually she was the one who slipped out in the early hours of the morning.

"I love your hair," Xal rumbled, twirling one ringlet around his finger. "It's very beautiful. As are you."

"I'm not perfect," Sera said cautiously, aware that he was making her feel all gooey inside, but unsure where this was going.

"Who is? If you were perfect, you would not be Human. If I were perfect, I wouldn't be Kordolian."

But you are perfect, she thought. At least, physically, he was. She wondered what sort of emotional scars he was hiding.

"You don't seem bothered by my scars," she pointed out. "Or my ink."

"In my culture, scars are a mark of honor. They symbolize painful healing, and there is nothing more honorable than that."

"Oh." His response surprised and warmed her. She was too used to getting pitiful looks from strangers, or being asked what had happened to her. Xal did none of that. He simply accepted that they were a part of her.

"And your tribal markings are beautiful. They're much more intricate than what Kordolians are capable of."

"My tatts?" She laughed. "The 'tribe' I belong to doesn't approve of this kind of thing. The tatts are all my own doing."

"But they're symbolic, aren't they?"

"I don't know about your planet, but on Earth, if you leave something out in the wilderness for long enough, nature will take it, and replace ugliness with beauty. I got the idea after seeing a hollowed out bomb shelter that had been reclaimed by nature, overgrown with vines. That was when I realized that even broken things could transform."

"The difference is that on your planet, things grow." Xal's look turned distant. "On my planet, everything is frozen, even society."

"But you guys are here, aren't you? I'd hardly call that 'frozen.'" Sera reached out and tilted his chin so that he was looking at her again. "And come on, be honest with me now. You're not really here for the 'females' are you? I mean, you seem plenty experienced, and that's a compliment, by the way."

Xal shook his head. "It's not as you think. I haven't been with so many females, as you might believe. I spoke the truth earlier. I wouldn't lie to you, Sera. Our race is dying. For some reason, females aren't born anymore. Our scientists, as powerful and knowledgable as they may be, have failed to find a reason for this. Sometimes I think the Goddess has decided to punish us and has kept all her daughters with her in the infinite plane, preventing them from crossing over." Sadness tinged his voice. "We used to be a noble race, but this curse has destroyed our people."

"No it hasn't." Sera pushed a stray tendril of hair away from his face, tucking it behind a pointed ear. "Look at you and the General, risking everything to protect a world you barely know, because you choose to hold on to hope. I don't know how you guys figured out that Humans were a match for you, but if it's true, then your people will survive."

"But first we have to make sure we don't destroy Earth. I fear I've dragged your entire civilization into disaster."

"So what if you have? You're going to get us out of it, aren't you? We've been defenseless for centuries, Xal. If not Kordolians, some other alien species would find us eventually. I'm starting to think we're better off with you guys protecting Earth than some cruel overlords from another planet." She narrowed her eyes. "You *were* serious about the protection bit, weren't you?"

"Of course." He still looked troubled. "But sometimes I wonder if it would just be better for us to retreat and leave your people alone. We Kordolians are a destructive species, both to others and to ourselves."

"So you'd leave us to be a sitting duck for the Evil Empire and those horrible giant insects?"

"I can't do that. But at the same time, I'm afraid of what might happen to Earth. Your people are vulnerable, Sera. Humans are a peaceful race. You're not equipped for war."

"Peaceful?" Sera scoffed. "What the hell makes you think Human beings are peaceful? Things aren't so bad now, but if you knew what we've done to one another throughout history, you wouldn't call us that. There are just so many of us that I think we take each other for granted."

Xal closed his eyes, a look of pain crossing his face. "You Humans don't know how lucky you are."

"Then you need to make sure we stay lucky."

When he opened his eyes again, they were clear and free

of anger. "I will make sure the Imperium doesn't threaten Earth again. But, as with all things Kordolian, it will be difficult."

"May I send a report to Earth? I'm sure my father and his cronies are freaking out."

"Not yet. I don't want any misinterpretations, and I don't want any opportunities for back-door deals between the Humans and the Empire. They are not to be trusted."

"Fine. But you have to keep me in the loop." What he was saying made sense. The wrong information in the wrong hands could lead to some pretty stupid outcomes. She knew of some Humans who would sell out to the Imperial Kordolians if they thought there was a profit to be made out of it.

People could be stupid.

Xal rested a large hand on her bare ass, feeling the smooth curves of her butt and thighs. "You will most certainly be kept in this 'loop'."

"Good to know, Prince, good to know." He was full of secrets, and Sera was getting the sense he was a conflicted soul. But she had managed to unravel him a little, and on the upside, she'd made him promise he would take care of Earth.

It had only taken mind-blowing sex for that to happen.

Now they just had to figure out how to break a galactic stalemate before all hell broke loose.

XAL HAD REQUESTED a meeting with Tarak and his five commanders, waiting until Sera slept before he stole out of his quarters, leaving her naked and tangled in the sheets.

To his amazement, his head was clear, the headache having disappeared, along with the irrational anger that had clouded his thoughts. And once again, he felt he could find a way forward, even if he still wanted to rip Luron Alerak's beating heart from his chest.

Sex with Sera had been incredible. Now he was beginning to understand why the General kept his female close. A part of him wanted to return to his quarters and do her all over again.

She had made him lose control in the most primal of ways, stripping back all the formalities and barriers until there was just the two of them; a man and a woman, responding to each other's desire.

The attraction had been mutual.

Something inside him had snapped he saw her on the floor, pinned under another male. He had been unable to process that scenario.

The urge to claim her had been overwhelming, and he'd given in.

Some royal he was. His father had always complained that he'd been too impulsive. He'd just proven that for a fact.

They were gathered in a dark, windowless room some-where in the bowels of the warship. The commanders looked to their General for guidance, mostly ignoring Xal. The military under Tarak's command were fiercely loyal to the General in a way that Xal hadn't quite yet grasped.

All Xal knew was that Tarak had worked his way up through the ranks in the most unconventional manner, so much so that he had caught the attention of his father, Emperor Ilhan. And when Tarak had started winning impos-sible battles because his aggressive fighting style and uncon-ventional military strategy, which was starkly different to that of the other Generals, Emperor Ilhan had declared him the new face of the military; the change Kythia needed to ensure the survival of their Empire.

Amongst the military, he was a living legend.

Some superstitious soldiers had refused to fight under any other command except Tarak's.

The Nobles hated him because he threatened their care-fully constructed hierarchy, where positions were granted as a birthright, and not won through merit.

The High Council despised him.

And somehow, a single Human female had undone all his father had sought to achieve. Now they were forging a trail none of them would have ever thought possible.

"We are at an impasse," one of the commanders, a slender Kordolian called Iskar said softly. "The Empire wants its Fleet Station back. They are desperate, otherwise they wouldn't have sent a battle cruiser this far from Kythia."

"I say fuck it." Jerik, a short, muscular commander with a head as smooth as polished stone thumped his fist on the table. "We bomb the shit out of them and deal with the consequences. If we act all soft on this one, they'll keep coming, thinking we're weak."

Tarak was leaning back in his chair, watching them all without saying a word.

"They'll destroy Earth out of spite if we do that." Commander Mardok glared at Jerik. "Do you really want the destruction of another planet on your hands?"

"The other glaringly obvious question is, where the hell did they come from? Did they map an alternate route?" Tarkun, with his braids, proudly worn in the Aikun style, raised his eyebrows.

"They're stretched thin, though." The fifth commander, Ikriss, ran a hand over his cropped white hair. "They won't risk sending any more battle cruisers, because that would leave Kythia vulnerable. Remember, we've just reduced their fleet to half."

"It seems we have to make some tough decisions," Jerik growled, as they all turned towards Tarak.

The General regarded them all in turn, his face an unreadable mask.

Xal caught his eye, a hint of a smile tugging at his lips. "So let's give them what they want most," he said.

They all turned to look at him in surprise. Xal didn't usually participate in military strategy; his job was to play nice and talk nicely with the natives. Out of all of them, he was apparently the most diplomatic, and that wasn't saying much.

"What do you mean, Prince?" Tarkun inclined his head respectfully.

"Exactly what I said, *avarth*," Xal replied, using the Aikun word for brother. "We give them what they want most. We give them the Fleet Station."

The General was staring at him, his crimson gaze unwavering. But a hint of a smile was playing on his lips.

"Ridiculous," exploded Jerik. "We can't surrender our military advantage to the Kaiin-cursed Nobles. That's a death wish. You might as well go back to Kythia and beg them for an execution. They'll come back with everything they've got and slaughter us."

"I'm suggesting we give them the Fleet Station," Xal said coldly. "Not the *fleet*. Why would we need an orbiting station when there is a perfectly good moon here?" He turned to Tarak. "How long would it take to empty the Fleet Station, strip it of all valuable components and rig it with enough explosives to destroy a reinforced Alpha Class battle cruiser?"

"It can be done before Daegan's warship reaches it. You intend to lure them into a trap."

"That's exactly what I'm thinking."

Tarkun, Iskar and Ikriss nodded in agreement, Mardok shook his head, and Jerik stared at him in disbelief.

"You will need to convince them to leave Earth's orbit."

"I'll do my best 'mad prince' act. The Nobles already think I'm mad, so it won't be hard to believe. I'll pretend you and I had a disagreement, and that I want to be re-instated in the Court. I will beg them to return me to Kythia in exchange for revealing the location of the Fleet Station. They can do a surveillance check to confirm it. When they reach it, we put up a bit of a fight, trick them into thinking they've defeated us, and give them the Fleet Station."

"They will kill you when they found out they've been betrayed."

"Ah. But they will have to deal with the entire Fleet Station being rigged with explosives. All I will need is a strategically placed escape pod."

Unexpectedly, Jerik burst into laughter. "It's actually a plausible plan, and spoken like a true Kordolian. Maybe you are your mother's son after all."

A warning growl escaped Xal's lips, and the Commander blinked.

"Did something make you think I wasn't a true Kordolian, Commander Jerik?" Xal's voice was low and menacing.

The Commander paled, holding up a placating hand. "Sorry. That was a stupid thing for me to say. But what stops us from simply going after them and blasting the shit out of them once they are outside the firing range of Earth? Are we ready to sacrifice the Fleet Station? That's a lot of Callidum right there."

"Pursuit is an option, but it is not without risk. Luring them into the Fleet Station would be most ideal, because we could simply eliminate them without any collateral damage. The Fleet Station has undergone much degradation after traveling so far, and we lack the resources to maintain it properly. It will eventually turn into space junk, so it is not unreasonable to sacrifice it." Tarak leaned back in his chair, considering the possibilities. "The alternative is a firefight between two Alpha-Class battle cruisers. It would get dirty, and we risk leaving Earth undefended during that time. It's a risk I'm willing to take, but either way, Xal would still need to convince them to leave." The General narrowed his eyes. "Xalikian, this is a dangerous plan, but not without merit." Tarak leaned forward. "Are you sure you are willing to take such a risk?"

"I won't allow them to win, General. And if you see to the details and arrange my retrieval, I have every confidence we will succeed. I am only one individual, and my life is no more valuable than those of the thousands who serve you."

Tarak nodded. "We will have to work together to persuade them that the Fleet Station is ripe for the taking. Easy enough. You will convince them that you wish to betray me. If it's Alerak and Daegan, they will believe what they want to. The fools are gullible enough." He regarded Xal with his unsettling deep-red gaze. "I will do everything in my power to ensure you get out of there alive, my Prince."

"I know, General Akkadian. That is why I have no hesitation."

"Then it is decided. You will lure *Ristval V* away from Earth to the Fleet Station, and we will arrange for its destruction." Tarak's expression turned grim, and a deathly silence fell upon them. They all knew what this meant.

Their actions would cause the deaths of hundreds of Kordolians.

It was the terrible price of war.

Tarak broke the stillness by pounding his fist on his chest once, in the traditional Kordolian military salute.

Xal nodded as the Commanders stared at him in shock. The General didn't salute anyone, *ever*.

But he had just acknowledged his Prince.

And Xal wondered how far the Imperium had strayed from its path that a Kordolian like Tarak could betray it.

CHAPTER EIGHT

When Sera woke, Xal was gone. She lay in the shadows, tangled in impossibly soft sheets, listening to the sound of total silence.

The bed wasn't really a bed, but more of a dark, organic cocoon; a rounded pod that was either stifling or cosy, depending on one's preferences. She stared up at the blackness, wondering what the hell had just happened.

Oh yeah, amazing sex, that's what.

Her stomach growled, and she hazily remembered her original mission, which had been so conveniently sidetracked. She was starving.

She slipped on her clothes and ran a hand through her disheveled hair, trying to make herself look presentable. The only thing she wasn't able to put back on was the g-string Xal had torn.

Oh well; she wouldn't be needing that anymore, anyway.

Sera headed for the door, only to find that she was locked in. The stupid thing wouldn't open, and as far as she could see, there wasn't any release panel. She stepped back and looked around. Xal's room was similar in size to hers, with identical furnishings. She would have thought he'd have something a bit more opulent, considering he was a Prince and all, but she was starting to find out that his title and his role in the Universe weren't so straightforward.

Sera collapsed back onto the bed, a tumult of thoughts running through her mind. She was sure Xal hadn't meant to lock her in, it was just that those weird doors were complicated, and only designed to admit or release the main occupant of the quarters. Feeling restless, she decided to explore the quarters, tapping panels here and there and running her hands across the smooth, curved walls.

Kordolian things were so strangely designed.

Sera brushed against a triangular set of blue lights on the wall and another basket-weave door opened. Inside was a narrow space that looked like some sort of closet, and beyond that was a washroom.

There was a smooth, dark cubicle in one corner, and when she poked her head inside, a torrent of cold water fell from the ceiling.

Sera jerked away in surprise, and the water stopped.

It was a shower.

How the hell were the Kordolians so liberal with water onboard a spacecraft that probably hadn't seen land in months? On the few Human space stations Sera had been to, they had always been on water rations, or they had been required to dry-cleanse.

Nothing compared to a long, hot shower. It was one of the luxuries of living on Earth.

Sera undressed and stepped into the shower, letting the water hit her in a cold blast. She shivered, turning her face upwards. There was no control panel to regulate the temperature. Apparently, Kordolians liked their showers cold.

Sera closed her eyes and let the frigid water cascade over her face. Cold water was better than a dry-shower, any day of the week, and the arctic temperature was actually helping her wake up and feel refreshed.

Especially after a session of wild, frenzied lovemaking with a certain silver-skinned alien.

She needed to get her head back into reporter-mode. She couldn't afford to be wandering around in a lustful daze, dreaming of fucking Xal all day long. She was supposed to be objective here.

Sera laughed. Objective was out the window.

It was bad enough that she'd already broken her golden rule; it was downright unprofessional.

But when she was faced with a sexy Kordolian who seemed to be equally as attracted to her, what was a girl supposed to do?

Ignore him?

She wasn't that virtuous.

Despite the cold shower, heat started to burn through Sera at the thought of his touch, and before she realized what she was doing, she'd slipped her fingers between the moist folds of her pussy, stroking herself.

Oh, come on, she told herself. *Just a little bit more.* She was locked in the dark chambers of a Kordolian Prince, onboard an alien warship orbiting Earth. It wasn't as if she could flick on the holoscreen and watch Netcom all of a sudden. She had to do something to pass the time.

Xal had awoken her long-buried sexual appetite, and it was like rain in the desert after a long, hard drought. She didn't know what the customs of his people were when it came to sex and relationships, but she felt as if she might pursue him to the ends of the Earth to take this further.

There was so much to explore.

Goosebumps rippled over her skin, and she opened her eyes, blaming the cold water. But when she looked into the shadows, her eyes touched upon amber, and she gasped.

"How long have you been standing there?"

He'd been watching her. That dirty, sexy bastard.

Xal stepped forward, a slow grin spreading across his handsome features. "Was I not sufficient for you, Sera?"

She blushed, having been caught in the act. "No, you were perfect. But you locked me in, Xal. What did you expect me to do? Clean the bathroom?"

"My apologies. I forgot about the Qualum door. I will have it re-programmed."

Sera looked at his plain robes and suddenly felt very naked. Which was stupid, considering she'd just been naked with him a few hours ago. But the way he was staring at her, with his predatory gaze, was making her conscious of her bare skin.

"Although, if being locked in here means you will spend your time pleasuring yourself in the shower, then perhaps I will keep you here for myself and enjoy you."

"Don't get full of yourself, Prince." Sera flicked water at him, but the cold droplets didn't make him flinch. Before she could react, he dropped his robes in a blur of movement and stepped into the shower.

"Can't you make this water warmer? How do you do cold showers all the time?"

"We like the cold," Xal murmured as he moved behind her, bending to nuzzle her neck. He tasted her skin with his warm mouth, and she pressed her slick, wet body into his, feeling his erection nudging against the small of her back. He brought his arms around her, capturing her breasts in his large hands. The sharp points of his black fingernails retracted like a cat's, and he traced his fingertips over her skin, fondling her nipples, causing her to shudder.

Suddenly, the water didn't seem so cold anymore, and Sera forgot she was hungry for food.

A different kind of appetite had been awakened.

"Let me take over with that, female," Xal whispered, his lips grazing her ear. He nibbled her earlobe, trailing soft kisses down the side of her face. His hands slid down the lean planes of her belly, gliding over her hips and around her ass. He brought one hand to the front and curled two fingers over her pussy, pushing them deep inside. Heat pooled in her belly and spread through to her core. "To leave you unsatisfied is most dishonorable."

He wrapped his other arm around her belly, drawing her into him. She found herself pressed against the hard planes of his body, their wet skin molding together. He was oh so warm, and his cock was nestled up against her, impossible to ignore.

Impossible to resist.

At this rate, Sera would never get any work done.

Xal stretched her, his fingers moving back and forth insistently, causing Sera to squirm against him. He held her tightly, trailing slow, hot kisses along her neck.

He moved his other hand up to caress her taut nipples, one at a time.

Sera moaned, planting her hands on the wall, pushing back against him. She bent over, and he slowly withdrew his fingers, eliciting a moan of pleasure.

He teased her entrance with his cock, its moist tip parting the silken folds of her pussy. Sera reached behind and took his length into her hand, guiding him.

He plunged deep inside her as she anchored herself against the wall of the cubicle. Water streamed over both of them, and a low, rumbling growl escaped Xal as he held her tight and fucked her slowly, his hands cupping her breasts. He was gentle at first, then he went faster, taking her deep and rough, their lean, slick bodies moving together. Sera let out soft sighs of satisfaction that became progressively louder as Xal pumped his hips, stoking her to new heights of pleasure. As he moved inside her, he planted a long, deep kiss on her neck, at the point just above her collarbone.

He ground his hips, his movements becoming more forceful, more intense, a possessive, primal sound issuing from his throat, mingling with her soft cries. He thrust deep, and he thrust hard, and his lips were on her neck, and he was kissing her there, and fucking her so hard and she wanted to come.

Oh, how badly she wanted to come. Yet at the same time she didn't want this to end.

The tension built. Her pleasure grew, becoming ecstasy. He stretched her and caressed her and claimed her. They moved to their own wild rhythm, and his grip on her became tighter and tighter, his mouth hot and demanding on her bare, wet skin.

Xal was insatiable. He took her higher, and he went even faster, and smoldering embers of sensation became a wildfire, and Sera writhed and arced her back, and then he came, slamming into her with a tremendous cry, his sharp fangs grazing the skin at her neck, drawing out a feeling of of exquisite pain.

The sprinkling of pain mingled with a tidal wave of bliss, sending Sera into overdrive as she orgasmed, slamming her fists against the wall.

Xal drew her against him, pulling her upright as she became a boneless, quivering, hot mess.

The tension drained from her body and a satisfied sigh escaped her lips.

Xal withdrew from her and she turned to face him, loving the way his expression had become so peaceful, a contented smile dancing on his lips.

"That wasn't exactly what I had in mind when I stepped into the shower," she said, as the water held them in its cold caress.

"I was just finishing what you started, female," he rumbled, looking most pleased with himself. "How could I leave you to pleasure yourself when I'm right here?"

Sera laughed as he rested his hands on her waist, gently stroking her skin. "Yes, how could you?" She pulled him out of the shower, examining the pulps of her fingers. They had started to look like prunes, from prolonged exposure to water.

"At this rate, we'll use up all of Silence's water supply, and I'll shrivel up like a raisin."

"Again, I don't know what that is, but you don't need to worry about the water. It's recycled in an infinite closed loop, constantly being filtered. All moisture onboard Silence, even vapor, goes back into the system. We will never run out of supply."

Sera shook her head. "You know, when you guys finally settle on Earth, you'll become overnight billionaires selling your technology."

Xal raised an eyebrow enigmatically, but said nothing.

Sera wrapped her arms around her naked body as the cold water dried, rubbing the skin of her arms where goose-flesh had appeared. Xal said something in Kordolian and suddenly heat radiated from the ceiling and the bathroom became dry and warm, the moisture disappearing in an instant.

He wrapped her in his own warm embrace. "You Humans don't like the cold, do you?"

"And you guys do?"

"Our planet is cold. It's our natural environment. But the warmer climate of Earth doesn't bother us. It's just your infernal sun and its ultraviolet light. Our eyes are sensitive to it."

"Remind me to get you a pair of sunglasses when we get back to Earth." Sera slipped on her clothes and shot Xal a wry look. "So was this all part of your plan, Prince Kazharan?"

"What do you mean?"

"Did you mean to bring me all the way up here and seduce me so I would write nice things about you and your Kordolian friends in my magazine?"

He looked shocked. "I would never use sex to manipulate you. That is sacred. Do Humans do such things?"

"Relax, Prince." She laughed. His earnestness was heart-warming, somehow. "I was just teasing you. I'm a big girl. A little bit of sex won't change what I write. And just because you're a skilled lover doesn't mean you're off the hook."

"You think me skilled, then?" He raised an eyebrow.

"Silly man, you know it already. You're clearly experienced in that department, so you don't have to sugar-coat your past. I get it. You're a Prince. It comes with the territory."

Xal smiled, but there was a hint of sadness in his eyes. "I know how it must look, Sera, but my upbringing wasn't a conventional one. I truly have very little experience with females. As a Kordolian male, I received training in the art of pleasuring a woman. It's a rite of passage for us."

"Oh." Sera was floored. "I'm sorry. I didn't—"

Xal took it all in his stride. "It must seem strange to a Human, coming from a planet where one can easily find a mate. But on Kythia, with our imbalance of males to females, we do everything we can to keep them satisfied. And Kordolian females don't conceive without reaching climax. It's essential for the release of certain hormones."

Sera bent and retrieved Xal's robe, draping it across his shoulders. He straightened her grey top, pulling a tucked-in bit from the waistband of her trousers, running his hands over her body, unable to help himself.

A contented sigh escaped Sera, and they made their way back into the sleeping area. Xal was silent and pensive, watching her with an unreadable gaze.

She observed him in turn, savoring his angular beauty and the fluid grace of his movements.

"Something's bothering you," she said eventually, reading into his silence.

"You've witnessed the conflict we Kordolians are facing with our brethren from the Empire. You saw the perpetrators first-hand. Our plans have changed, Sera. Soon I'll have to leave here to deal with it once and for all."

"Well, I'm shadowing you, so—"

Xal put a finger to her lips. "No. The place I'm going is too dangerous for a Human. You will return to Earth and await word from us."

"What do you mean, dangerous? I've been to war zones before, Xal. I'm sure I'll be fine, as long as—"

"No." His eyes became hard, like chips of glass. "Absolutely not. There's no place for you where I'm going, because those I'll be dealing with might easily kill you or torture you or enslave you, purely because you're Human. I won't *ever* put you in that kind of situation, Sera Aquinas."

She stared back at him in shock, because it was as if he'd transformed in front of her. Gone was the cheeky, cocky, passionate male who'd just made love to her. In his place was a regal Kordolian Prince whose word was absolute.

Xal, she was beginning to realize, was a man of many faces.

"My story isn't finished," she said quietly, withdrawing from his touch. "At least allow me to stay here, onboard *Silence*, until you return." She paused. "You *will* be coming back, won't you?"

"I intend to," he said cautiously, but there had been a tiny hesitation there, and she sensed there was a lot he wasn't telling her.

"You're going to them, aren't you? You're planning to do something to those enemy Kordolians."

He remained silent, and that infuriated Sera. That meant that whatever he was planning was stupid or risky, or a combination of the two.

"Why don't you want to tell me what's going on, Xal?"

"You will know if I succeed," he said softly. "Then you will have your story, Sera Aquinas."

For some reason, that statement filled Sera with cold dread. "You're coming back, right? I mean, this isn't some sort of weird goodbye, is it?"

"Sera." His eyes softened then, turning the color of a fading sunset; amber shot through with streaks of tawny brown. "I'm not doing this alone. I have every faith in

General Akkadian and the soldiers under his command. But I can't predict the will of the Goddess. Sometimes she can be cruel. This time, I hope she'll be kind to me. I have every intention of coming back to you, Sera. Don't worry. I'll be fine."

"Idiot. You have to come back, or I'll kill you." Sera forced herself to smile, even though she was worried. It just so had to happen that when she'd finally found a man who accepted her, scars and all, and didn't give two shits about her family ties, he had to go off to save Earth from his own people.

The God of Irony was smiling down upon her.

To hell with going back to Earth. If Xal was going to be such a *male* about it and not tell her anything, she would have to use her powers as an investigative journalist and find out exactly what was going on.

The only problem was, she didn't know where to start. She was good at blending in on Earth, but onboard a warship full of Kordolians, she kind of stood out.

Perhaps that's where a little drone-cam or two might come in handy.

———————

XAL WATCHED in fascination as the nanite-infused tissue compound melted into the neat surgical wound the medic had made, knitting his damaged flesh together.

"Give it ten phases, then come back and see me for an epidermal patch. Don't leave it too long otherwise you'll start to form granulation tissue, and that might cause scarring. You're lucky. There's not so much of this stuff left. I'm down to my last batch." The medic, Zyara, applied a clear dressing with her gloved hands.

Xal looked at the healing tissue in the underside of his arm. A long cut had been made and a tracking device had been inserted. According to the General, it was a highly sensitive piece of technology, designed to be picked up over ultra-long distances.

There would come a time when Xal would need to make a quick escape from the Fleet Station, and Tarak, who intended to follow behind in a small, cloaked craft called a *stealth arrow*, didn't want him to get lost in the vastness of space. With the absence of gravity and so many forces involved, escape trajectories could become unpredictable.

Now he'd become just another blip in Tarak's vast network of assets.

Xal flexed his arm experimentally, feeling no pain at all. Zyara had numbed the area with a few well-placed electrodes, temporarily stunning the nerve endings.

She raised a lilac eyebrow as she peered at her holoscreen, scanning over a bunch of data Xal didn't understand.

The look she gave him was one-part astonishment, and two-parts amusement, her eyebrows lifting even higher. "You've been busy lately, Xalikian. I won't ask you about the details, but whatever you're doing, keep doing it. It's working."

"What are you talking about, Sirian?" He called her by her House name, causing her to frown. Zyara al Sirian was an oddity; a Kordolian female from a Noble House who had done the unthinkable and studied medicine. She was cool-headed in dangerous situations and had been hand-picked by Tarak to be the First Division's combat medic, much to the collective outrage of the establishment.

But in those days, no-one had argued with Tarak when it came to recruitment for the First Division. The elite unit of enhanced soldiers was his and his alone.

Zyara winked at him. "Have you been getting headaches lately? Or have you felt angry for no reason? Your hormones are displaying the *Zyllic* pattern. Severe Mating Fever with recent rapid resolution. As I said, whatever you're doing is working. I'll bet you feel fantastic right about now."

Xal stared at her in shock. "Mating Fever?"

"It's real, my Prince. And you've got all the risk factors. Young, athletic build, active lifestyle, intact horns, abstinence. It isn't really a disease. The modern classifications are all wrong. It's just evolution. Without the hormonal overload, our ancestors would have died out."

"So I'm not going insane?" Relief coursed through him.

"You don't look insane to me." Zyara shrugged and started to unhook the monitoring devices from his body. Xal shook his head in disbelief. The medic was right. He *did* feel fantastic, and it was because he had given in to his desire. Sera had been incredible. Even now, the memory of her scent lingered, and he longed for her warmth, the feel of her strong, sinuous body and the sound of her low, husky voice.

He'd loved the way she'd sounded, her voice melting him as she expressed her satisfaction. He'd loved the way she looked at him, with dark, burning desire in her brown eyes.

Zyara's monitor started to beep gently, and she shot him a sidelong glance. "As I said, Mating Fever. And it seems you've found a cure. I'll leave you to whatever you're thinking about right now." She looked slightly amused. "The monitors don't lie." She ripped the remaining electrodes from his bare chest.

Xal shrugged, not in the least embarrassed by her observations. Thinking about Sera made his heart beat faster; it was true. "As you said, it's evolution." He stood, rubbing the dressing on the inner side of his left upper arm. The area was numb and cold, and all he felt was a faint tingling as the nanites did their work. "I'll be back in ten phases for the skin patch. I'm just relieved it's not the royal madness."

"Xalikian," Zyara handed him his robes. "I don't think that kind of madness is hereditary, and there are many who think your mother is totally sane. There's no medical diagnosis for what she has, so stop looking over your shoulder for shadows that aren't there."

Xal stood and dressed. Level-headed Zyara, of course, was

the epitome of common sense. So why were there still lingering doubts at the back of his mind?

He forced himself to shelve them.

"This Mating Fever," he said. "Will it come back? Is there a permanent cure?"

"It's unpredictable." Zyara removed her gloves and entered some data. "Some get it worse than others. It usually fades over time as a male ages and his hormone levels drop. But as far as I know, the best way for you to keep it at bay is to have regular intercourse."

An image of wet, hot, naked Sera flashed through his mind.

Xal shook his head, trying to curb his arousal. His fear of hereditary madness had been replaced with another kind of madness.

He was becoming obsessed with this Human, and he was certain now that it wasn't just because she was one of the first few Human females he had encountered.

He was attracted to her inquisitiveness, her strength, and to the intelligence that gleamed in her dark eyes, not to mention her sinful, lithe body. She had jumped at the opportunity to come aboard *Silence* without hesitation or demands. She had asked questions and taken initiative.

And when it came to acting upon mutual attraction, she hadn't been shy.

She'd been the first to make a move, and he'd loved that.

There had been concern in her eyes when he'd hinted at his plans. She was actually *worried* for him.

To a Human who didn't understand the complexities of the Kordolian Empire, his plan would probably seem ridiculous and terrifying. He really didn't know how to explain it all to her.

So he'd kept quiet.

Now he just had to pretend to betray his General, get

onboard the enemy ship, and somehow convince them to leave Earth's orbit.

Sera would resent him for leaving, but in time she would understand, because he would do everything in his power to return to her.

And then, without the imminent threat of the Imperium looming over them, they would be free to explore her fascinating planet, and each other.

CHAPTER NINE

After Xal slipped away to attend to some mysterious business, Sera munched on the cube-shaped goodies he'd retrieved for her, astounded at the complexity of flavor that had been packed into such tiny bite-sized morsels.

Veronian food, he'd called it, and he'd been so certain that she'd enjoy it.

He'd been right. Damn him.

She was back in her quarters, sitting on her bed, adjusting the settings on a tiny surveillance drone. She'd put it on night-vision mode, and she was about to let it fly off to find her target.

Of course, that was Xal.

He'd be mad if he figured out he was being followed, but her drones were designed for stealth and silence, unlike the standard models, which emitted a soft buzzing noise.

Something big was going down, and for some reason, Xal didn't want to tell her much.

The big idiot thought he was doing her some sort of favor. She was starting to get the impression that despite being an Imperial Prince from an evil, technologically superior race of alien super-beings; a complicated guy with a complicated past, he was just a big softie at heart.

Oh, she still had questions, and lots of them; her journal-istic brain never switched off. But didn't think Xal had any ill intentions towards Humans.

Sera walked over to the door with the tiny drone in her hand. The door opened and she stuck her head out into the corridor, peering left and right. It was empty. Good.

She released the drone and it disappeared, drifting up into the darkness, its tiny, internal motors propelling it along the passageway.

Sera slipped back into her room, the door fusing shut behind her. That door and its weird technology creeped her out, but at least she knew no-one could enter her room without her permission. She retrieved her monitoring pad and peered at the screen, watching as footage from the drone appeared.

It sped down the corridor, keeping close to the ceiling.

The night-vision was awesome. Details she hadn't noticed before came to life, and she realized that this giant, deadly structure the Kordolians called *Silence* was an intricate mesh-work of black materials, fused and woven together without any visible bolts or welding.

Sera popped another little cube in her mouth as the drone showed her a dimly lit, cave-like entrance. She navigated it inside and realized it was some kind of medical facility. Various monitors and equipment were installed along the walls. There was a large chair in the centre, with tubes and wires alongside it. A large circular tank filled with liquid domi-nated the centre of the room, a soft glow emanating from it.

A Kordolian woman wearing long, white robes stood before a holoscreen, entering data. According to Xal, Kordolian females never went off-planet. So who was this statuesque beauty?

Beside her, Xal was fixing up his robes.

Huh? Why was he in the medical bay? Was he unwell?

The woman gave him a tube of something and Xal took it reluctantly, a stubborn expression crossing his face. Sera turned on the sound, and was grateful for the translator clipped to her ear.

"It's fibrogel." The woman, who Sera presumed was a medic, advised him. "Apply it to your cuts and scrapes every ten phases, especially the one on your horn there. Otherwise, they may fester. And in future, you might want to take it easy in the simulation room."

Xal responded with a noncommittal grunt, taking the medicine. Sera rolled her eyes. Males. They thought they were invincible.

"You *will* use that medicine, you big idiot," she said, more to herself, because he couldn't hear her. One way or another, she would make sure of it.

Xal farewelled the female medic and left the room. Sera fumbled with her monitoring pad and commanded the drone to 'lock' onto him. She felt a little bad for spying on him in this way. It was a huge invasion of privacy. She had always tried to use the micro-drones as little as possible, and only when absolutely necessary.

But this time, the fate of Earth was at stake, so she felt justified enough in her decision.

Anyway, if something *really* sensitive came up, she could always shut it off. She'd already seen Xal naked, so she figured he didn't have much more to hide.

Xal left the medical facility and veered off down a narrow passageway Sera didn't even notice until he turned into it the last second. He walked for a while, the corridor seeming to go on forever. He didn't pass a single soul.

Obviously, this wasn't a thoroughfare so often travelled by the Kordolian personnel.

He walked and walked until he came to a small door which unraveled, admitting him into another room. This one had a port-hole with a view of the stars and the familiar blue-

and-green outline of Earth. Sera realized he must be on the underside of the ship.

Xal sat in front of a holoscreen and activated it, entering a string of commands.

"Contact *Ristval V*," he ordered, and the holoscreen came to life.

"Patching you through, Highness," a gentle, mechanical voice said, as the Kordolians Sera had seen before came into view.

"You are alone this time, Prince Xalikian." The gaudily dressed Kordolian with the rings and makeup smiled, his fangs peeking over his lower lip. It was a cold smile that didn't reach his eyes. "Does this mean you've finally come to your senses?"

"I have considered your request," Xal said quietly. "You are right, Luron. This course of action we are taking is futile. I have observed the Humans, and they are nothing like us. I cannot live here."

"Inter-species mating is an abomination," Alerak spat. "A disgrace to the Kordolian race. We can't allow our blood to mix with that of an inferior species. Humans will be useful to us in other ways, but not as mates." A look of disgust crossed his features.

"You are right, of course." Xal's expression was so glacial that Sera shuddered. "I have come to realize that after spending a short time on Earth." He shook his head. "It isn't the way forward for the Empire." Xal leaned back in his seat, steepling his fingers and returning Alerak's glare with an implacable stare. "I cannot promise you everything you have asked for, Luron, however I am willing to offer you a deal. I have thought long and hard about mother's offer, and I consider it fair. If she is willing to forgive my past crimes and allow me to return to the Court, I will forget past vendettas and return to my rightful place at her side. In exchange, I will give you the location of the stolen Fleet Station."

Sera breathed in sharply. She couldn't believe what she

was hearing. The Kordolian she saw through the tiny lens of her surveillance drone was a cold, terrifying stranger.

This wasn't the Xal she knew.

What was he doing?

Alerak raised a manicured, silver eyebrow. "So the prodigal son wishes to return to mother's embrace. I am tempted to believe you, Xalikian, but I need further proof of your loyalty. How do I know you're not hatching a plan with the dreaded General? You can, of course, understand why I am being wary. Your past actions shook Noble society to its core."

"I am coming to you with information that will get me killed if Akkadian finds out about my betrayal. You know how he is. Do you think I would risk my life if I were toying with you, Alerak?" Xal snorted in disdain. "However, I can understand your wariness, so I am willing to co-operate. What do you require of me, Luron?"

"Bring me the Human owned by Tarak al Akkadian as proof of your intentions. Even the General is not exempt from the rulings of the High Council. She has been claimed as the property of the Empire, and he will have to learn what happens when he tries to steal from the Empire. He seems quite fond of that female. We will destroy this thing he has fought so hard to keep."

The Kordolian's voice was devoid of any emotion, and a strange, fanatical light had entered his eyes. Sera's skin crawled. He was talking about the General's mate, Abbey, as if she were an insect he could easily crush. Humans were nothing to these Kordolians.

Xal's expression was blank; he didn't react in any way to Alerak's cruel proclamation. "It will be difficult," he said finally, his voice a bleak monotone. "You know how Akkadian gets. I am risking my life by coming to you with this information. I would think that someone in your position would consider my offer a most generous one. You wish to recover the

Fleet Station, and I am dropping it into your open hands. Would you risk it all for one Human?"

Alerak managed to look slightly pained. "Your offer is fair, Prince. However, the Infinite Mother has specifically requested the Human, and I cannot disobey her. Find a way to bring her to me, show us where the Fleet Station is, and I will grant you passage back to Kythia."

"You ask a lot, Luron."

"You want to go back home? Then find a way to deliver what I ask. That is all." The image of the Kordolian wavered and flickered, before disappearing.

Xal took a deep, shuddering breath and leaned forward, dropping his head into his hands.

From her hidden vantage point, Sera blinked in confusion. Her head was swirling with conflicting thoughts, and she couldn't believe what she had just witnessed.

The Prince was conniving with the evil Kordolians to sell out the General and his people.

That couldn't be right. Something didn't add up here.

What had happened to the sweet, sensual male who had treated her with such tenderness and given her pleasure beyond her wildest dreams?

The Xal she had seen just now had seemed every bit as cruel and dispassionate as the Imperial Kordolians. He hadn't flinched when Alerak had demanded Tarak's mate.

Either he was a cold-hearted bastard, or he was a very, very good actor.

Either this was all part of some grand master-plan, or he really was going to sell the General out. The latter would spell disaster for Earth.

Sera had to find out for certain.

She would confront him and find out the truth. Because she couldn't believe that the man she had just seen and the Xal she knew were one and the same.

Because no-one, alien or Human, could have faked what had happened between them.

XAL FOUND the General training a group of young soldiers in the simulation chamber. Tarak was standing impassively behind an observation panel, watching them fight.

They were bruised and bloody, breathing heavily from exertion, their clothes disheveled and torn.

The General didn't go easy on anyone.

"It didn't go exactly to plan." Xal came up beside him, staring out at the Kordolian soldiers as one of them landed a vicious, low kick on his opponent, earning a satisfied grunt from the General.

"What do they want?"

"They want me to bring Abbey to them as proof of my true intentions. The Empress wants to make an example of her."

Tarak swore viciously in Kordolian. Some of the terms were so colorful that Xal winced. No-one swore quite like a soldier. "Deluded imbeciles. Alerak and Daegan are asking for death. Your plan was elegant and effective, Xalikian, but we will have to find another way."

"I know."

Sensing something, Tarak turned, his red gaze fixing on something above. "We have a visitor," he growled. The General leaped up and snatched something out of thin air. He opened his palm to reveal a small robot-like device. A tiny red light blinked back at them. It was a recording device of sorts.

"What are you doing, Human?" Tarak glared down at the thing, his ears twitching in irritation.

"Sera?" Xal blinked, staring at the object. It was most definitely Human in design. "Have you been following me? I told you not to worry."

He expected Tarak to be furious, but to his surprise, the

General just looked at him with a resigned expression. "This is to be expected, Xalikian. You should have known when you invited her on board. I would do the same thing if I were in her position. You need to decide what you want to do with her."

Xal should have been angry, but the thought of Sera spying on him only made him aroused. He smiled at the faint ridiculousness of it all. She was the only one who could get away with something like that. As far as he was concerned, she could observe him any time. He sighed, taking the tiny recording device from Tarak's open palm. He examined it, noting the small, retractable lens and rotating metal blade that allowed it to fly.

The only problem was that he now had to explain himself. "Now you see what I had intended," he said, looking at the lens. He wondered if she could even hear him. "Did you watch me when I was conferencing with Alerak? You probably thought I'd gone mad. In truth, I was going to trick them into leaving Earth by pretending to betray Tarak. We figured the promise of the Fleet Station would be too juicy a prize for them to ignore. Unfortunately, Alerak made an impossible demand. So the plan is off." His shoulders slumped, and Xal rubbed his temples. Fatigue was starting to kick in, and the headache was back, a dull throb behind his eyes. "Never mind. We will figure out another way."

The bot winked silently at him, it red light flicking on and off in a steady rhythm. Xal stared back at it, trying to picture Sera's reaction. "Clearly, this is going to be more long and drawn-out than we had anticipated," he said, unsure whether he was saying it more for his own benefit, or for hers. "I will try to distract Alerak and eventually, another opportunity may present itself. But it's not going to be the quick solution I'd hoped for. I'm sorry you're not going to get the report you wished for, however I think your time spent here has given you a good grasp of the situation, and our true intentions. You may return to Earth whenever you wish."

Behind them, the observation panel shook as one of the Kordolian fighters was thrown into it, his body slamming against the thick wall. He recovered his footing and faced his attacker, wrestling him to the floor. Tarak nodded in approval.

Xal frowned into the lens. "I can imagine you will want to talk. I will be up shortly."

And with that, he dropped the strange Human device into one of his pockets, wondering how in Kaiin's hells they were going to hold back the rest of the Kordolian Empire without any further bloodshed.

CHAPTER TEN

She wasn't surprised when the panel next to the door chimed. Xal's face appeared on the screen. "Let me in, Sera."

She moved in range of the door and it slid open. The Prince stood before her in all his Kordolian glory, a worried expression on his face. Even when his mouth was turned down in a frown and his eyebrows were drawn together in concern, he was gorgeous.

Sera was expecting him to be angry. She held up her hands. "I can explain," she began, but he put a finger to her lips.

"Don't. I should be angry with you, but I understand. If my planet were potentially being invaded by another race, I would spy on them as well. But it's irrelevant now. The plan won't work. I will not endanger Tarak's mate."

The look on his face tugged at Sera's heart-strings. Unable to resist, she moved close to him, taking his warm hands into hers. "So let me get this straight. You want to trick these guys into leaving Earth by leading them into a trap, but if you don't give them Abbey it won't work, because they won't believe you're legit."

"That's one way of putting it, yes."

"Then give them Abbey."

"What are you saying?" He recoiled in horror. "You can't seriously be suggesting—"

"I'm horrible, huh?" Sera grinned, and Xal's eyes widened in shock and confusion. "Do they even know what Abbey looks like?"

"Well, no, but—"

The wildest thought had occurred to her. The enemy Kordolians wanted the General's mate. If Xal wanted his plan to work, he needed a Human female as a bargaining chip, didn't he?

The General would never give up Abbey as bait. Sera had seen the kind of man he was and the way he looked at his mate and she knew that for a fact. But Sera was available. There was a chance the Imperial Kordolians didn't even know what Abbey looked like. Sera could very well become the single factor that would convince them to leave Earth.

Could she do such a wild, crazy, reckless thing?

Xal's people were as scary as hell, but Sera had always been a jump first, ask questions later kind of girl.

"I'll be your Abbey. You'll be the evil Prince Kazharan. We'll get onboard the *Ristval V* and carry out this devious plan of yours. All they're expecting is a Human woman, right?"

Xal managed to look relieved and aghast at the same time. "Absolutely not," he snapped. "Are you out of your mind? You've seen how dangerous they can be and how little regard they have for the lives of Humans. How can I let you walk into such a nightmare?"

"Xal, my planet is going to ruined if we don't do anything. Millions, if not billions, could die. How can you stop me from trying to defend my home? Besides, you'll look out for me, won't you?"

"It is out of the question," Xal growled. "I won't put you in such danger."

Sera grabbed Xal's horns and pulled his head down until

their lips were almost touching. "The only problem with that statement is that you don't own me, Xalikian. And I'd rather put myself in mortal danger with you than sit back and wait until you guys end up in an all-out war, with Earth stuck in the middle. So let's do this thing."

"You'd be willing to risk your life?"

"For Earth. For Humans. For you. But I'm not suicidal, Xal. I think your plan is gutsy, and there's a damn good chance it could work. You will just need to convince your evil buddies that you want to keep me by your side. Make something up; I don't know, claim me or something. Just don't let me out of your sight. I know you'll figure something out, because you're a freaking good actor. You almost had me believing you were an evil bastard back there."

"It wasn't difficult." Xal looked into her eyes, and she saw a swirling storm of emotion cross his face. "I just drew on what already exists inside me."

"You did what you had to do." Sera shrugged. "We all have a dark side, Xal. It really all comes down to what you decide to do with it."

Exhaling, he ran a hand through his hair. "You're impossible, Sera Aquinas."

"So are you, Xalikian Kazharan." She brushed her lips against his ever so slightly, and drew back, releasing him. His mouth was half-open in shock.

"Would you really do this? I would have to treat you unkindly in order to make them believe the lie. I would hate myself for doing it, every step of the way."

"Do what you have to do, Xal. I know you would never truly hurt me. You're too much of a big, ol' teddy bear to do anything horrible."

"Teddy bear?" His eyebrows rose. "More human terminology I don't understand?"

"We can even do a role-play to practice beforehand, if you

want. I'll be the helpless Human captive and you'll be the evil alien Prince, spiriting me away to your dark planet."

Xal looked both horrified and amused.

"But somehow," Sera continued, in a mock-theatrical tone, "the evil Prince falls for his beautiful Human prisoner and she develops a hopeless case of Stockholm syndrome, because of course, he's a handsome devil, and they end up craving each other's touch. By the time they reach his planet, they realize that they've fallen in love."

Xal was staring at her with his mouth agape, his fangs showing. "The General was right," he whispered, shaking his head in disbelief.

"What are you talking about?" Sera wondered if she had taken it a little too far. But the thought of Xal taking her captive, even in a pretend scenario, was getting her all hot and flustered.

"All Human females are crazy." He ran a hand through his moonlight colored hair, looking exasperated. "Erratic, unpredictable, illogical."

"Sensible and practical is more like it." Sera snorted. "Don't you dare treat me like I'm some pampered princess."

He closed his eyes, a pained expression crossing his face as he shook his head. "No," he said finally, looking at her again. "I can't let you do it."

"You would risk war because of me? Don't be stupid, Xal." Sera's voice rose, ever so slightly, betraying her frustration.

"You would recklessly endanger yourself, putting yourself into an impossibly dangerous situation, just because that idiotic Alerak demands a Human female?" Xal's features had taken on a stubborn cast, and he loomed over her with anger simmering in his golden eyes. His voice had risen a notch. "I would rather start a war than allow them to touch you. In the past I've lost people very important to me. I can't bear to go through that again. I've just found you, Sera Aquinas, and I can't bear to lose you."

Sera matched his anger with her own. "And who are you to decide whether I'm being reckless, your Highness? Maybe I was being reckless when I walked through the door of your house back on Earth. Maybe I was being reckless when I decided to come with you onboard *Silence*. Maybe I was being reckless when I decided I wanted to fuck you. But that's what I do, Xal. People have called me reckless my entire life, but I just do what I think is right."

She took a deep breath and clenched her fists. "I'm still here, aren't I?" She was full of tension. Oh, what she wouldn't give for a good old-fashioned sparring session right now. She could really spend some time hitting the pads. "You need to put your fears aside and let me do this," she said slowly. "You need to make a choice. Are you going to let things from your past get in the way of what you know is a damn good plan? Back on Earth, you told me that you wanted to see Kordolians and Humans as equals. What is it, Xal? Are we equals, or do you consider yourself superior to us, and to me?"

He looked at her long and hard, not saying a word. She got the feeling he was deliberating. Inside him, a conflict raged. For a moment, she caught a glimpse between the cracks, as deeply held pain flickered in his eyes.

Then, unexpectedly, she was being pushed back, Xal's strong hands grabbing her wrists, holding them over her head as she found herself pressed against the wall. He was able to restrain her with just a single hand, holding her wrists together. Shocked, she tried to resist, but his grip was like iron.

Fuck, he's strong!

He leaned in and kissed her then, wildly and passionately, pressing his hard body against hers. Sera melted underneath him, responding to his kiss as she felt his erection brushing up against her.

He was insatiable, and she didn't mind at all.

He broke away, staring at her with an intensity that made

her burn. "If you are to be with me, you *will* be a princess, and you *will* be pampered. No objections, Sera."

Damn him. He said the most panty-melting things at the worst times and she loved it.

"The truth is, that if you join me pretending to be a Human prisoner and we board the enemy ship, I'm terrified at what I might have to do to you to keep up appearances and I'm terrified I will give us both away, because there's no way I could be cruel to you."

Sera inhaled his woody, masculine scent, no longer struggling against his restraining hand. Her arms were still pinned above her head, but Sera was starting to enjoy this position. "Well I'm more afraid of you guys and the bad guys having a shootout with Earth as target practice. So suck it up, big boy. I'm tougher than I look."

"You had better be, my helpless captive."

"So I'm coming with you, right?" She gasped as he slid his free hand into her pants, finding her moist, sensitive entrance.

"I am still thinking about it, crazy woman. Somehow, you are starting to convince me," he growled, "in more ways than one." He shook his head.

"I get the feeling you'll make a *great* evil Prince."

His lips brushed against her ear. "I can be as evil as you want, Princess." He said it so menacingly, in his low, smooth-as-silk baritone, that she actually shuddered with anticipation. She found it oh, so deliciously sexy. He kissed her at the base of her neck and slipped his fingers deep inside her pussy.

"Oh yes, please," she sighed, helpless to resist her dark Kordolian Prince.

CHAPTER ELEVEN

The General looked at both of them, a skeptical expression on his face. "You're saying she wants to accompany you pretending to be Abbey, because those imbeciles think they can lay their hands on *my* mate?" There was barely restrained rage in his voice.

"Daegan and Alerak have never seen Abbey. They don't know what she looks like They are only expecting a Human female, and as far as they're aware, Abbey is the only Human female onboard *Silence*. So if I go to them with Sera, they will believe I have turned against you, because no-one in their right mind would betray you and think of ever returning. And then, our plan will be set in motion."

"You approve of her doing this? It will put her in immense danger."

"I don't approve at all. But I acknowledge her right to contribute to the defense of Earth, and I will use all of my wits and cunning to ensure she does not suffer at their hands. After all, I have something they want, and that gives me power. I will set conditions. I will tell them I wish to deliver her to mother personally, and as such, she is my personal property until we reach Kythia. They will have to believe it, otherwise the deal is off."

Tarak turned to Sera. "You do not have to do this, Human. We can find another way."

Sera shook her head. "What's my life compared to the eight billion lives on Earth? Besides, I'll have Xal with me. He'll keep me safe and you'll be following us, right? It's actually a simple plan when you think about it. We get to the Fleet Station, eject in escape pods, you come rescue us and *boom*. No more Fleet Station. No more evil Kordolians." Sera looked at both of them, her gaze settling on Xal. "I'm well aware it might not go to plan. I'm well aware I might end up enslaved or dead, but I'm the only Human right now who has a chance to make a difference, and there's no way in hell I'm going to sit on my ass and wait for Earth to get bombed to bits. If I did nothing now and that happened, I'd never forgive myself."

She said it with such certainty that Xal was moved. She was willing to risk her safety for the future of her people. What had he done to make this clever, brave female trust him so?

If she was willing to go that far, then he had to put his own fears aside and let her do this.

Tarak assessed both of them with a cryptic expression on his face. His eyes dropped to the two tiny red points where Xal's fangs had broken the delicate skin at her neck. He raised an eyebrow, but said nothing.

He turned to Xal. "I personally would not allow Abbey to do such a thing," he said in Kordolian. "I would prefer to wage war rather than see her fall into their hands, but I am selfish like that."

He must have forgotten that Sera still wore the translator. Or maybe he hadn't.

One never knew with the General.

"My first instinct was the same," Xal replied. "But she has made her point. Sera is fully aware of the dangers, and I mean no disrespect, but I am more flexible than you, General. She has made her decision as a Human who wishes to protect her own planet, and I will respect it, even though all my instincts scream against it. With her help, we might just have a chance to pull this off. If I think at any point that she is in serious danger, we will abort the mission. I will put her in an escape pod and get the hell out of there."

Tarak glanced at Sera. "Are you absolutely certain, Human?"

"For the hundredth time," she growled, "I said I'm doing it. I'm just waiting for you men to curb your protective instincts, as sweet as they may be, and let me do my thing. I've taken a few hits in my time, General." She laughed. "You have no idea."

Tarak gave Xal an appraising look. "She is stubborn and reckless. Some would say foolhardy."

"Yes." He nodded in agreement.

"Impulsive, unrealistic."

"I know."

"But she is brave." There was grudging respect in the General's voice.

"I'm right here, guys," Sera shot them an irritated glare. Xal loved the way her brown eyes flashed, full of intelligence and defiance. He wondered where her inner strength came from. Even when she was the sole Human on a ship full of Kordolians, she demanded to be treated as an equal.

Since he'd first encountered her, she'd been unwavering and resolute.

Humans were a fascinating species, indeed.

Xal vowed then and there to do whatever it took to keep her from harm. It would be a difficult balancing act, trying to ensure the success of their mission, while at the same time keeping her close. But he had spent enough time in the Palace of Arches to know the minds of the Kordolian Nobles, and one such as Luron Alerak could be easily manipulated.

The Nobles on Kythia were so caught up in the belief of their own superiority that they responded to flattery and ego-stroking with almost childlike naiveté at times. They responded even better to cruelty and a firm hand.

And even though he had attained the rank of General, Daegan had spent very little time in the field.

Xal suppressed a grim smile. If he wasn't so concerned about Sera's safety and in turn, his own sanity should anything happen to her, then this little escapade might even turn out to be fun.

CHAPTER TWELVE

They were sitting in a small two-person transport, gliding soundlessly through space. The stars became a blur as they sped up, heading towards the enemy Kordolian warship, the *Ristval V*.

Xal had told her disdainfully that it was named after a long-dead Kordolian Emperor.

The transport was automatically piloted, since neither of them knew how to fly. Sera felt a bit like a lamb being led to the slaughter.

But she had chosen to do this, and she trusted Xal.

It was strange. They had known each other for such a short time, and yet she felt so comfortable around him, even though he was from another planet. She felt more comfortable with him than she did with most Humans. People on Earth always acted differently around her once they found out who her family were.

As they moved further away from *Silence*, a blue bolt of plasma shot past them at an impossible speed, sending shock waves through the cabin. An alert sounded, and the tiny transport veered, changing trajectory and speeding off at a different angle.

"What the actual fuck?" Sera spluttered, her heart in her mouth.

Another bolt shot past them, this one grazing the body of the transport. The craft shook, and Xal grabbed Sera's shoulders as they dropped to the floor.

"What the hell is going on?" Out here in open space, they were practically defenseless.

"Relax." Xal was inappropriately calm. "It's a ruse. I told Tarak to fire a few distraction shots at us, to make them think we're escaping. The transport's defensive avoidance system has kicked in. Even if they were serious, the further we get from *Silence*, the harder it is to hit us. We're such a small target, after all, and this thing's avoidance system is one of the most advanced in the Universe."

"A little warning next time," Sera gasped, as Xal helped her up from the floor. The transport had stabilized and increased its speed, the stars turning into an endless stream of white as they shot towards the enemy cruiser. A few more streaks of blue light shot past, disappearing into the vastness of space as their craft dodged a stream of asteroids.

She glanced at Xal, taking in his appearance. He had ditched his casual robes for a regal black uniform. He wore a fitted jacket with a high collar and long coat-tails over a pair of simple black trousers that were tucked into knee-high black boots. The collar was embroidered with intricate red motifs. The largest and most prominent was an image of an eye, reminding her of an ancient Egyptian hieroglyph.

His long, wild hair was neatly tied back into a high topknot, accentuating his obsidian horns. At his side, a long, wickedly curved black sword was sheathed.

Sera wondered if Xal really knew how to use the weapon, or whether it was just a ceremonial thing. She suspected he was deadly with it.

The outfit was severe and intimidating, but Xal wore it comfortably, as if he were accustomed to it.

"What?" He noticed her staring at him.

"I like a man in uniform," Sera grinned, raking her gaze over his tall figure, checking him out.

Xal gave her a flat look. "I fucking hate this uniform," he grumbled. "It's stiff, uncomfortable, and ridiculous. It's got Kordolian Empire written all over it. But one has to keep up appearances." He returned her appraising gaze with a heated look of his own. "I'd imagine yours is a little more comfortable."

"It's okay." Sera shrugged. She was wearing what apparently passed for a slave's uniform. It consisted of a stretchy, form-fitting white top with long sleeves and hidden pockets, over a pair of white leggings. The clothes were seamless and designed for ease of movement. Unfortunately, they didn't leave much to the imagination. Small, soft shoes covered her feet, made from a flexible but durable synthetic material.

She'd left the Kordolian translating device in her ear. It was hidden discreetly beneath her hair, which was left out, a mass of wild curls cascading over her shoulders.

Tarak and Xal had gone over what to expect and explained how she was supposed to behave.

She was supposed to pretend to be terrified of Xal, and do whatever he said.

Xal had looked rather uncomfortable when Tarak had explained that part.

"Do all Kordolians have slaves?" The enemy warship came into view, looming larger in their line of sight. Like *Silence*, it look as if it was capable of massive destruction.

Xal nodded. "Any non-Kordolian species on Kythia is considered subservient. Aliens that are brought to Kythia are sorted and sent to different households based on their perceived value and overall physical grade. The Noble Houses get the pick of the slaves, and the rest go to the ordinary folk."

Sera shuddered. The thought of intelligent life-forms being sorted like cattle chilled her to the bone. "So basically that's it," she concluded. "They're then forced to live their lives out as slaves."

"Generally, yes. However those who demonstrate particular value or trustworthiness may receive a small stipend, to spend as they wish, and brief periods of leisure time. They are then classed as Servants. Only the most liberal households grant Servant status to slaves. Many Nobles disapprove of the practice."

"And you, Xal?" Sera asked quietly. "What do you think of your people's culture of slavery?"

"I abhor it," he said vehemently. "I grew up in the Palace, where the worst abuse of slaves takes place. I've seen everything my people are capable of, Sera."

"So what makes you think differently, Xal? I mean, you don't just grow up in a culture like that and change your mind overnight."

"My opinions formed over time." He took her hand into his and started absently running his fingers over her grazed knuckles, which were healing. "I'll admit, I was like them at first. But things happened to me." He uncurled her fingers, entwining his with hers. His hand engulfed hers, and his palms, just like hers, were callused. "Though you don't need to know about all that. Just know that I would never enslave a Human, or any other race, no matter how I'm about to behave. I want you to remember that, Sera."

"I know that, Xal." A warm feeling suffused her as he kissed her battered knuckles, one by one. "You're too much of a big old sweetie to do anything like that."

His laughter was bright and clear, like a bell, his fangs flashing in the starlight. "I'm glad you think that, Sera. No-one else would say such a thing. I've certainly never thought of myself that way."

Sera grinned. "So don't be shy and do what you have to do. I won't hate you for it. You'll just have to make it up to me afterwards."

"Aren't you afraid, Sera?"

"I'm shit scared," she admitted. "But reminding myself how scared I am isn't going to change anything. The way I deal with my fear is to ignore it. That's what I've always done, ever since an accident I had as a kid. It's a character flaw, but it's who I am."

Xal kissed the back of her hand, inhaling the scent of her skin. "Thank you," he said softly, "for being brave, and understanding. And sorry, for what I'm about to do to you."

Sera didn't have time to say anything in response, for the giant docking bay of the *Ristval V* had just started to open, and they were about to step into the enemy's lair.

Xal produced a set of black metal restraints. "Hands behind your back," he whispered. "They're just for show. I'll leave them unlocked."

Xal's gentle hands caressed her wrists briefly, followed by the sensation of cold, hard metal. He snapped the restraints on her, and Sera tested her bonds.

"They will come apart if you pull hard enough," he murmured. His hands came to rest on her shoulders. "I'm going to place something around your neck now." His voice was tinged with disgust. "It's a punishment collar. I've put it on the lowest possible setting, so you should feel only a gentle buzz against your neck if I activate it. When that happens, you need to act as if you're in pain. Again, I'm not going to lock it."

The collar went around her neck, and Sera froze. Even though it was only pretend, it still felt strange to be restrained like a Kythian slave. She spared a thought for the poor aliens who suffered at the hands of their Kordolian masters and decided she never wanted to set foot on Kythia.

For once in her life, she was speechless.

Xal seemed to sense her nervousness, because he placed a reassuring hand on her shoulder and kissed her on the cheek. "Don't worry," he said, staring straight ahead as the transport floated into the docking bay. "I'll take care of you, Sera."

Then he moved away, a cold expression settling across his features.

A light, lingering touch on her thigh was the only hint of his true feelings as they crossed the threshold into enemy territory.

SERA FOLLOWED Xal down the ramp, walking behind him and keeping her eyes downcast. From the corner of her vision she could see a row of Kordolian guards, all dressed in black. She tried to keep her shoulders loose and relaxed, because having her arms restrained behind her was proving to be quite uncomfortable.

The guards stood to attention, stamping their boots in unison as Xal passed.

"For the Eternal Imperium!" Their low voices echoed in the vast docking station as they shouted some kind of traditional Empire salute. Sera was grateful for the translator clipped to her ear. She would have felt a hell of a lot more vulnerable if she didn't understand what was going on.

Xal strode arrogantly across the walkway as if he owned the entire ship, and she struggled to keep up with him. They were met by a small entourage of Kordolians who greeted Xal by bowing in a ridiculous manner, making funny, swirling gestures with their hands.

"Prince Kazharan." One of the Kordolians, a male wearing long orange robes, greeted him. Sera recognized him as the psycho guy called Alerak. "We are most grateful that you have found enlightenment and returned to the embrace of the Infinite Mother. She has yearned for the return of her most favored son, and she hopes you will return to your rightful place at her side."

"The Imperium is wise, Councilor Alerak," Xal replied, his voice ringing throughout the cavernous space. "She is ever-merciful and all-powerful, and I have had time to see the error of my ways. I will return to her, and the Court. I understand now that mother was only acting in the best interests of the Empire when she sent my unfortunate child into the cold, everlasting embrace of the abyss. For in death, comes mercy." His voice was bland, almost nonchalant, revealing no hint of his true feelings.

Sera froze, horror spreading through her. Xal had mentioned something before about his mother killing children.

No way. Could it be? Xal's own child?

She couldn't imagine anything so monstrous.

If her suspicions were correct, then Xal was being incredibly composed to stand up in front of these Kordolians and speak so coldly, as if he had seen the error of his ways.

"I see you have brought the Human," Alerak continued. "This is Akkadian's creature?" He walked over to Sera and took her chin into his fingers, tilting it upwards so she was looking into his yellow eyes. She did her best to appear afraid, casting her eyes downwards. His fingernails were sharp, and they dug slightly into her skin, causing small pinpricks of pain. He laughed. "*This* is the thing Akkadian fought the High Council for? The former General has gone mad. Ugly little thing. We shall take it and process it so it is fit to present to Empress Vionn."

"Take your hands off my property, Alerak." Xal put a possessive hand on Sera's neck, pushing her away from the other Kordolian. The movement looked brutal, but he was ever so gentle. "I have claimed it as the property of House Kazharan. I will be the one to present it to mother, as penance for my wrongdoing. You will not touch what is mine."

"But I was ordered to bring the Human to her directly," Alerak protested, his voice going up an octave.

"I've seen what you do to your slaves," Xal snarled, looming over Alerak with real hatred in his eyes. "I am aware that mother wants to punish Akkadian, but I would have the

Human transported to her in one piece. The General shows affection towards it. I've witnessed it with my own eyes. We will devise a suitable torture once we reach Kythia, one specifically designed to enrage and humiliate both Akkadian and the Human. In the meantime, I want the Human to be presented to mother intact. Therefore, I will keep it and take this opportunity to break it in. By the time it reaches Kythia, it will be the perfect submissive slave. Do you have a problem with that, Luron?" He used Alerak's first name, and Sera got the sense that he was somehow being disrespectful.

If she didn't know better, she would have thought Xal was the most terrifying thing in the Universe right now. His transformation was so convincing that she shivered, glad that underneath all the theatrics, he was on her side.

"Fine." Alerak sniffed, waving one ring-encrusted hand. "The Human can be your responsibility. But you will have to accept the inconvenience of it staying in your quarters. The holding cells are full."

"I don't have a problem with that. It can sleep on the floor. Unlike you, Luron, I know how to discipline my slaves. I don't beat them to death." Xal curled his lip in disgust. "Besides, I have been without slaves for so long that I will enjoy having it attend to me for the duration of our journey."

"It's not as if there's a shortage of slaves," Alerak grumbled, looking sullen.

There was a loud crack as Xal backhanded him across the face, savage satisfaction crossing his features. The Councilor blinked at him in shock. "Wha—?"

"We do not waste, Luron. Even slaves aren't to be wasted. Senseless waste is frivolous and unbecoming. How do you think I tamed this one so quickly? Not too long ago it was given too much freedom. Akkadian was indulgent with it. But now it understands what will happen if it defies me. A little well placed fear is a lot more effective than excessive force, Luron."

"Y-yes, my Prince." To Sera's astonishment, Alerak looked up at Xal with something like adulation. It was almost as if the Councilor had enjoyed the slap. Faint scratches had appeared on his left cheek where Xal's sharp nails had torn the skin, a tiny trickle of black blood marking his cheek.

Weird.

These Kordolians were incredibly weird, and the atmosphere on this ship was oppressive.

It was different to *Silence*.

Silence felt like paradise compared to this madhouse. It was amazing what a bit of free spirit could do to a place. She was beginning to understand why Xal and General Tarak had left their home planet.

Xal regarded Alerak with a dark look. All the Kordolians were, on average, taller than Humans, but Xal towered over the Councilor, his horns adding to his impressive height. He looked so deliciously intimidating in his black Imperial uniform that Sera felt the faint stirrings of arousal.

Not again! This was happening far too often these days.

She stole an appreciative glance at Xal when she was sure no-one was looking, then reminded herself she was supposed to be playing the role of a terrified slave.

The Kordolian soldiers, who reminded her of henchmen, stared at her blankly as they continued on down the walkway. Their eyes, which were colored in varying shades of fire from yellow to deep crimson, but often a combination of the two, had the glazed look of rusted-on fanatics.

They believed in the greatness of their Empire, and everyone else was dirt.

That was the vibe she was getting.

Scary, indeed.

"So now," Alerak rubbed his hands together, scurrying up beside Xal, who walked at the front of the pack. "You will tell us the location of the Fleet Station, and we shall reclaim it in the name of the Empire."

Xal stopped dead in his tracks, turning to face the other Kordolian. "You would presume to rush me in my business like some common merchant?" His tone was soft and full of menace. "Have Court standards slipped in my absence?"

Alerak's shoulders slumped. Xal pressed home his advantage. "You will show me to my quarters, I will take my fucking time to settle in, and then I will summon you and General Daegan, to discuss our plans. Just because I have been in exile does not mean you can treat me like a commoner, Luron. And we do not discuss matters of the Empire in corridors like thieves."

Oh, he was playing this role magnificently. Sera stood in quiet admiration of Xal's acting skills, all the while wondering how much suffering he had gone through to become the person he was now.

Because so far, he had treated her with nothing but respect.

Even when he was pretending to be her cruel Kordolian master.

Alerak bowed his head in apology. "Of course, my Prince. I did not think. Forgive my haste. I will have you shown to your quarters."

"Make sure you remember your manners when I am onboard, Councilor," Xal hissed, his amber eyes narrowed dangerously. "Otherwise you may find out the hard way just how much I take after my mother."

The soldiers surrounding them made no effort to raise their weapons. Alerak paled.

He was afraid of Xal, but he was also staring at him with reverence.

Xal turned and looked at Sera, pinning her with his intense gaze. In the middle of this strange scenario, on an enemy ship surrounded by Imperial guards, he somehow managed to share a sliver of intimacy with her.

His eyes burned with desire, quickly hidden as he looked away.

Her eyes widened ever so slightly, before she dropped her gaze to the floor.

She walked forward, her heart pounding.

Their relationship was now a forbidden thing. That look could have cost them everything if Alerak had noticed. But he hadn't.

Adrenaline pumped through her, but she kept her expression blank, slumping her shoulders in defeat.

The way he'd looked at her had been possessive yet at the same time gently reassuring.

You're with me.

That's what he'd been saying to her, in the space of a single glance.

"Come, slave," he said aloud in Universal, with an imperious wave of his hand. "You belong to me now."

XAL SIGHED in relief once they were in his quarters, away from the harsh stares of the Kordolian guards. He tore the restraints off Sera's wrists, pulling her towards him. "Sorry you had to see that," he whispered. "I won't allow them to so much as look at you again."

Sera ran her fingers over the collar around her neck. Xal growled and ripped it off. "I hate these things," he spat, tossing it across the floor. "Such a barbaric device."

She looked up at him in wonder, once again reaching up to caress his horns. Xal shuddered as her slender fingers stroked the sensitive surface. She tenderly pushed a strand of stray hair away from his face.

"You're amazing," she murmured, confusing him.

"I was horrible," he muttered, closing his eyes as a pleasant sensation crawled across his skull, relaxing him.

"You were flawless. If I hadn't gotten to know you over the past few days, I would have been shit scared of you, just like Alerak was. He seemed equal parts terrified and awed. Being spoken to like that; it was as if he liked it but hated it at the same time. That was strange, Xal."

"He's a *temin*," Xal said flatly. "In Kordolian culture, there are those who become excited when they are treated cruelly, or when pain is inflicted on them. Alerak is a classic example. I just played to his base instincts. My mother slaps him around all the time, and he loves it."

That seemed to fascinate Sera. "What a strange and complex society you come from, Xal. The journalist in me is dying to pick your brains." She searched his face, her brown eyes glittering with curiosity. "But the lover in me wants to know you, Xal. I want to know all of you."

She was feeling him out, seeing how far she could go with him.

He wasn't ready for that. Xal pulled away from her. "There are things you're better off not knowing," he said darkly. "That perverse little glimpse of Kordolian life you had just now is enough. Believe it or not, I was once like them."

She glared at him. "Just because you've been there, doesn't mean you're a bad person, Xal." Sera pinned him with a look that threatened to strip all of his deepest secrets bare. "Back there you said something about a child," she said softly, cutting him deep, reaching a place he really didn't want to go to right now.

Xal held up a hand. "Don't." His voice was ice-cold.

Thankfully, she knew when to retreat, her soft, pink lips pressing together in a tight frown.

"I have to show my face on the Bridge," he said stiffly, turning away from her. "You're smart enough to know that you're not to set foot outside my quarters. Please don't get into a state where I have to rescue you from the holding cells, because I *will* risk everything to save you."

"Yes, master," she said ironically, her eyes traveling up and down his uniformed figure. "Don't worry, Xal. I won't be going anywhere."

Xal slipped out of the room, a strange emptiness filling him as he left his beautiful Sera behind. A part of him had wanted to reveal everything to her, but now wasn't the time.

He was playing a very dangerous game with these Kordolians, and he needed to remain sharp. He had something they wanted, and that gave him power, but he would slowly need to draw them into his lie.

Alerak was easy to fool.

General Daegan, on the other hand, was another matter. He wasn't as easy to fool, but Xal had sensed his weakness. Unlike Tarak, Daegan was a desk soldier; he commanded his troops remotely, rarely going off-planet. The fact that he was here in Sector Nine was a sign the Empire were desperate.

And desperation led to mistakes.

He would have to use all his wits and cunning to convince these Kordolians to withdraw from Earth and go after the Fleet Station, and General Tarak was about to give him a big helping hand to convince them.

Tarak had started withdrawing his fleet from the station and had ordered them to surround Earth. If Daegan were to see that the Fleet Station was unguarded, he wouldn't be able to resist the lure of capturing such a hefty prize.

Xal strode down the narrow corridors, heading in the general direction of the Bridge. He'd assumed *Ristval V* would have a similar layout to *Silence*, because Tarak told him they had both been modeled on the same prototype.

The soldiers he passed in the corridors looked at him with flat eyes, bowing in acknowledgement.

Xal ignored them, his skin crawling. Stepping onboard *Ristval V* felt like stepping back inside the Empire, with its bleak, painful memories.

The Empire was death.

They had taken two precious souls from him, and billions more from the Nine Galaxies.

Xal made his way past the residential quarters and found himself standing at a precipice, looking down over the command center of the warship.

He stood in a cavern-like opening, beyond which a narrow bridge extended out across the heart of *Ristval V*. Xal strode out onto the walkway, making sure his footsteps were heard as he looked down. General Daegan was sitting in the command chair, looking at a series of holoscreens. His subordinates were gathered around him, monitoring a stream of data.

They looked up at Xal in unison.

He stared down at them with an icy expression, not saying a word. Daegan spun in his chair. "Xalikian." His low voice reverberated around the space. "You have information for us."

"Daegan." Xal regarded him for a moment, trying to remember the sincere young commander who had been a friend to his father and had treated him with affection when he was a child. That man was long gone. In his place was a cold-faced, cynical soldier.

Daegan looked tired.

Xal leaned over the balustrade, raising his voice. "I don't trust you, Daegan, and I'm certain you don't trust me. What stops you from taking my head once you have the information you need?"

"I have an edict from the Empress, ordering me to bring you back alive. Your mother needs you by her side. Do you wish to see it, Xalikian?"

No! His first instinct was to refuse. But that would arouse suspicion. Slowly, he nodded, and Daegan brought up a holographic projection.

His mother stared back at him. The image was a shock to his system. Xal's mouth went dry and he gripped the balustrade tightly.

Hatred flooded through him.

Anger nearly made him tear the metal railing from its fixtures.

A pair of familiar crimson eyes stared back at him. The Empress Vionn's face was composed, almost serene, but her eyes held seethed with a deadly combination of power and madness.

Xal saw himself mirrored in her. The resemblance was unmistakable.

But his mother had aged since he had seen her last. The lines in her pale, silver skin had deepened, and her hair was shot through with black. She was still intimidatingly beautiful, but time was slowly asserting its authority, siphoning away her youth.

Xal fought hard to keep his expression neutral.

Seeing this perfect representation of the female he detested so much was a shock.

"General Daegan," she began, in a low, silken voice. "Your comrade is a thief. Tarak al Akkadian has stolen my Human, half of my military, and even my only remaining son." Vicious anger radiated from her, reverberating through her speech, making her eyes as hard as gemstones. "I need you to return what is mine. Bring me the Human, bring me back my Fleet Station and bring me back my son. Make it clear to Xalikian that he will be welcomed with open arms. My flesh has healed and all is forgiven. I need my heir, Daegan. Akkadian will learn the hard way what it means to betray me. I will take back everything he has stolen from me and then I will make him suffer. Do you understand me?"

Daegan cut the recording then, watching Xal carefully as the image of his mother flickered and disappeared. "Do you still think I would want to kill you, Prince?"

"I was only being cautious, Daegan." Vionn's yearning for an heir filled Xal with revulsion. There was no way he would ever sit on her cursed ebon throne, but he kept any hint of his true thoughts to himself.

"As are we, Xalikian. That is why we had you bring the Human; as proof of your true intentions. There are reports that Akkadian is quite attached to that female, although I have no idea why. There are suggestions he has even mated with it." His features twisted in distaste.

"It belongs to House Kazharan now," Xal said icily. "I will be responsible for training it."

"So I have heard." Daegan said coolly, eyeing Xal with barely concealed speculation. "You have claimed it, then?"

"The Human is mine now," Xal snapped, baring his fangs. "And I protect what belongs to me, even if it is a mere slave." It wasn't too hard to make that last statement believable. As with everything, there were elements of truth mixed in with the fiction.

"Hm." The General looked thoughtful. If he harbored any suspicion, he didn't let it show. "Well, my orders were to bring you and the Human back in one piece, so if you are intent on breaking it in, that is one less specimen for me to worry about."

Xal hated the way he was forced to talk about Sera. He hated the way these Kordolians spoke about Humans, dispassionately and coldly, as if they were animals. But right now, he had no choice.

He had to keep up the facade.

Fiction and truth.

He was capable of cruelty and ruthlessness if provoked. It was a character flaw.

"The Fleet Station is anchored in Sector Seven," Xal announced in a lazy drawl, before turning. He started to walk away. He waved a hand in the air. "Co-ordinates Jel-Kau-Vir-Sea-08941. Thinly guarded at the moment, I believe. Of course, you will still have to fight for it, but it's nothing the *Ristval V* can't handle. Run a scan through Imperial Surveillance and check it. If you are so desperate to claim back one of the Empire's jewels, you will set the most direct course for Sector Seven. Forget about Earth. There is nothing of value here. Leave General Akkadian to defend his precious Humans. The next move is up to you, Daegan."

"How do we know this isn't all part of Akkadian's master plan?" Daegan called after him. "How do I know I'm not playing right into his hands?"

"You don't." Xal turned, bleakly amused. "You have to account for that possibility too. You're a General, aren't you? That's what you're supposed to do. You can stay here in Earth's orbit, waiting for something to happen, or you can complete your duty by retrieving the Fleet Station and returning to Kythia. Remember, we have Akkadian's Human. He's bound to be angry. You had better think about leaving soon, because he's probably planning his attack as we speak. In this life, hesitation will cost you dearly, General Daegan."

Xal left the promise of glory and the fear of Tarak al Akkadian to sink in as he disappeared into the shadows.

CHAPTER THIRTEEN

After what felt like hours, they finally started to move. At least that's what Sera thought was happening. The whole ship seemed to vibrate, and she assumed that was the thrusters powering up. She couldn't be certain though, because she was in a windowless room and everything surrounding her was black. Kordolians seemed to dig the color black.

Xal had gone out again after dropping off some food. The brown gelatinous bars smelled like seaweed and jerky and Sera put them aside to attempt when she was really starving. She wasn't desperate just yet, and now she could understand why Abbey had been salivating over her ramen.

Imagine being stuck for months on a spacecraft with only that to eat? She shuddered.

Xal had said something about going to look for an escape pod, just in case they needed to leave in a hurry.

That was rather sensible of him. They were only on an enemy warship leaving Earth's orbit. Like, what could possibly go wrong?

Sera positioned herself in the centre of the room and started to go through the motions of a warm-up routine. They were heading to Sector Seven, according to Xal.

For Humans, that was a three-month trip, at best.

Kordolian spacecraft were faster, and after a long discussion with Xal trying to figure out equivalent units of time measurement, she estimated that on *Ristval V,* the journey would take about two weeks.

The speed this thing was capable of was mind-boggling.

But that meant two weeks cooped up in these dark, depressing quarters, and that could be a recipe for insanity. At least she wouldn't have to go out and face the creepy Kordolians, though.

She'd had quite enough of being looked at as though she were nothing more than a piece of flesh.

So she'd decided to try and stay fit, because even in the confines of the ship's quarters, there were a whole bunch of exercises she could do to keep herself lean and toned.

Sera propped herself up on one elbow on her side and started to do some hold crunches. After the first twenty, her body started to protest, but she continued, grunting with exertion.

There was something a bit surreal about what she was doing now, calmly going through her workout routine while they sped towards possible doom.

The physical movements helped silence that small, insistent voice at the back of her mind. It helped hold at bay the terror that threatened to take hold and paralyze her.

But she would *not* give in to her fear. Never again.

Never hesitate.

The spacecraft accident that had left her with terrible injuries had brought her close to death at a tender age. Ever since then, Sera suspected something in her had changed. Perhaps a part of her brain had been damaged.

Perhaps that's why she was here and not sitting on Earth, waiting for the inevitable.

She pushed herself through the remainder of her crunches

then switched over to the other side, a faint sheen of sweat appearing across her forehead.

That's when the doors slid open, and Luron Alerak stepped inside.

SERA FROZE, mid-crunch. The Kordolian official, or whatever he was, stared at her, outrage twisting his thin lips into a frown.

What the fuck is he doing here?

Slowly, Sera moved into a kneeling position, keeping her eyes downcast.

"What are you doing, slave?" He questioned her in Universal, his voice full of suspicion. Sera kept her head down, trying her best to appear fearful.

"Master wants me to keep my body well conditioned," she said softly, injecting a little nervous tremor into her voice. "He ordered me to do these exercises."

Alerak moved towards her, his orange robes swishing around him, his various bracelets and trinkets clinking as he walked. "What belongs to House Kazharan belongs to the Empire. That Human body of yours is designed to serve, slave." He placed a hand on her head, his fingers trailing through her hair. Sera fought to keep from recoiling in revulsion.

He smelled gross, too. Like a mixture of stale musk, patchouli and a faint note of rotting cheese.

Alerak ran his hand down the side of her cheek and tipped her face upwards. "Since getting on this infernal ship, I have not received my usual pleasure." His eyes roamed over her, trailing down to her body. "I'm so desperate right now I have even sought the company of a Human." He laughed in disgust. "As soon as I saw you, I knew I must have you. You are ugly, but you smell delicious." He bent and dipped his nose into her hair, inhaling deeply.

"I don't think Master would be very happy if you did that," Sera warned, remaining very, very still, even though she wanted to get up and smash him in the face.

"What the Prince doesn't know will not disturb him," Alerak whispered. "This will be between you and me, slave. Besides, who would believe a Human?" He parted his robes, revealing his scrawny grey body. His limp cock hung in front of her face, and Sera recoiled in horror.

No. Fucking. Way.

"Master will be very angry," she whispered. "He can get violent when he is angry. Please don't do this."

It was her last-ditch attempt to get this guy to go away. Because there was no way in hell she was going to suck his dick.

Alerak dug his fingers into her skull, and Sera winced in pain. "You are not to tell me what I can and can't do, Human. "Give me pleasure, or I will make sure you suffer the most excruciating of tortures once you reach Kythia." His voice became high-pitched. "You are a slave, Human. A slave! Do you really understand what that means? From now on, you do not speak to me; you do not so much as look at me. You will do what I say. Do. You. Understand?" His sharp nails were really starting to hurt her. Sera was sure he had drawn blood. "Do it now, Human, and make it quick." An urgency had crept into his voice, and Sera realized he was afraid Xal might return.

"Do it," he insisted, pulling her towards him by the hair. "Arouse me. Give me pleasure."

In a flash, Sera was on her feet. "Master told no-one is allowed to touch me, except him."

"Your master isn't here. How *dare* you talk back to me!" He brought his arm up to slap her, but Sera was faster, blocking his blow and twisting his wrist. His eyes grew wide in outraged disbelief.

She danced back out of his reach, resisting the urge to grin. "I'm only following my master's commands," she said in a deadpan voice. Alerak lunged for her. Sera sidestepped and made a dash for the sleeping pod, where the wrist restraints lay.

She grabbed them and delivered a low kick to Alerak's shin. He roared in pain and tried to grab her. He was probably much stronger than her, so she just had to keep out of his reach. If he couldn't lay a hand on her, he couldn't harm her.

She had the speed advantage, and this guy was no warrior.

Sera kicked him again, managing to hit the same spot, and this time he became unbalanced, falling to the floor, his orange robes swirling around him. A jewel fell from one of his bracelets and clattered across the floor.

"How dare you," he screamed, as Sera swooped in and snapped the restraints around one of his wrists. He flailed and she lost her grip, the metal device swinging in the air. He was trying to stand, but she scrambled on top of him, pinning him down in a grapple. She didn't have much time, because as soon as he moved, he would overpower her.

Sera reached across and snapped the other end of the restraint around his ankle, tying him up like a pretzel. She heard a click, and she hoped to hell the device had worked.

Alerak tried to free himself, but the restraint held fast, and he screamed in outrage. "You will die for this, slave!"

He tried to stand, but with his right wrist tied to his left ankle, it was impossible. Sera stepped away, squatting down at a safe distance so she could look him in the eye. "Master told me that no-one else should lay a hand on me," she said sweetly. "I'm just following his commands."

To her horror, he had a raging erection. Fucking pervert.

"Besides," she added, unable to help herself. "You've become aroused, just as you asked. You like being treated this way, don't you, Kordolian?"

Alerak's yellow eyes burned with hatred. "Release me this

instant, Human filth! I will flog you for this!" His jewelry clinked as he thrashed on the floor. With his free leg, he kicked uselessly into the air.

"I can't disobey Master," Sera said innocently, picking up the punishment collar and turning it idly in her hands. "And I don't know how to take them off."

"You are dead, Human!" Alerak stopped writhing about when he seemed to realize it was futile. The bonds couldn't be broken. "You just wait until we reach Kythia. The Empress will tear you apart."

"Hm." Sera simply looked at him, shrugged and turned away. She was probably in big, big trouble, but this creep had asked for it.

The worst thing about it all was having to spend time confined to quarters with this hysterical, repulsive idiot.

She hoped Xal would get his ass into gear and come back soon.

WHEN XAL RETURNED to his quarters, he found Alerak trussed up on the ground like a *vorchek* that was about to be roasted, one wrist bound to his ankle with the slave restraints.

The punishment collar was around both of his ankles, acting as a restraint and rendering him immobile.

Sera sat on the bed, an innocent expression on her face. She didn't say anything, instead shrugging and pointed to Alerak, who had his back turned to her. She made a questioning gesture with her hands.

Alerak spluttered in outrage when he saw Xal. "Release me, Kazharan," he shouted. "Look what this Human has done to me! It must be killed. This is completely unacceptable."

Anger made his hands shake. His gaudy robes were undone, and underneath, Xal saw that he was naked.

Xal instantly understood what had happened, and white-hot rage burned through him. He wanted to tear Alerak's head from his shoulders.

Instead, he squatted down in front of Alerak. "You are trespassing," he said softly. "For what reason do you come into *my* quarters and try to touch *my* slave?"

"You see what it has done to me," Alerak hissed. "This is unacceptable and I demand punishment. The High Council will hear of this, Prince."

Xal slapped him hard. Alerak reacted by blinking, and Xal saw that he had an erection. He shook his head in disgust. "What would I punish her for? She was obviously carrying out my will in my absence. Although I would have been a little less gentle with you."

"I am a Noble of the Kordolian Empire, and it has dared to raise a hand against me. Even death would be an inadequate punishment for this wild animal. I would demand it, at the very minimum."

Xal raised his hand again, and Alerak trembled in anticipation. In truth, he wanted to punch him in the face, and it was taking every ounce of his self-control to hold himself back. "Tell me Alerak," he said, slowly lowering his hand. "What would I list as the official reason for execution? What is the crime? Singlehandedly defeating and restraining a Kordolian Noble?"

Alerak's pale yellow eyes burned with shame and hatred. "It tricked me," he spat. "It fought dishonorably."

"Shall I call the guards to remove your restraints? I'm certainly not inclined to touch your filthy skin."

"No!" The Councilor desperately waved his only free hand. Of course, he wouldn't want anyone to see him in this state. The rumors that followed would be brutal. "That won't be necessary. Just get me out of this, Kazharan."

Xal looked up at Sera, who was smirking. Clearly, she could handle herself. But he was angry that she'd been put in this situation in the first place.

The High Council publicly denounced inter-species mating, but everyone knew that many Nobles fucked the help behind closed doors, and Alerak was no better.

He'd obviously thought he could have his way with Sera. Slaves were usually too terrified to do anything.

"What should I do with you, Luron? Shall I haul you out into the corridor and leave you for the cleaning bots to sweep up?"

"If you dare to publicly humiliate me I will report you to the High Council, Kazharan. Just because the Infinite Mother wishes to show you mercy does not mean you can walk back into the Court with all your privileges re-instated."

Xal smiled then, baring his fangs. "I'll tell you what, Luron. I won't tell anyone of this if you won't. If I let you go now, we will resume our usual business and you will forget about this unfortunate incident. In exchange, this shameful display of your incompetence will remain between you and me."

Unseen by Alerak, Sera winked at him.

Alerak looked up at him in helpless fury. "At least discipline your slave," he whined.

"What for?" Xal raised an eyebrow. "She has not disobeyed me. You, on the other hand, tried to violate what is mine." His hand dropped to the hilt of the Callidum sword that hung by his side.

It had been his father's, and although it appeared ceremonial, it was very, very sharp.

Xal unsheathed the blade. Alerak paled. Sera raised a curious eyebrow.

In a single, fluid movement, Xal sliced through Alerak's bonds, the blade whispering past his exposed skin. Alerak scuttled backwards, his eyes full of fear.

"Cover yourself, Councilor," Xal growled, "and get out of my sight."

CHAPTER FOURTEEN

"Am I in trouble?" Sera stood to greet Xal as soon as Alerak left the room. "Have I just blown your cover?"

"Forget about that." Xal pushed her hair away from her eyes, carefully evaluating her appearance. "Did he hurt you?"

"No." She shook her head, her eyebrows drawing together. "I tried to hold back, but he wanted me to-" she shuddered, "to pleasure him."

Xal snarled, looking as if he were about to commit bloody murder. "He needs to be punished." He went for the door, his sword still in hand.

"Xal, stop." Sera curled her fingers around his sword hand, stilling him. "You have a bloody temper, don't you?"

"When it comes to you, I do." He slowly sheathed the blade, embers of anger smoldering in his eyes. "This won't happen again."

Sera wrapped her hands around his horns and started stroking them. That always seemed to calm him. "You need to have a clear head right now."

Xal closed his eyes and shuddered. "I can try and think things through objectively, but there's only so much I'll tolerate when it comes to your safety. It was reckless to allow you to do this. How did you manage to convince me to bring you along, female? You must have put a love-spell on me." He placed his warm hands around her neck, stroking her soft skin. Electric ripples of pleasure shot down Sera's spine, pooling in her belly, sending out tendrils of arousal that unfurled in her core.

How did he have this effect on her, each and every time?

"You are a fighter; I knew it." He put his lips to her forehead, leaving a soft, lingering kiss. "You brought that spineless idiot to his knees and trussed him up like a pitiful *vorchek*."

"I don't know what that is, but I'll admit, I lost my temper. I'm sorry I kicked his ass."

"No, Sera. Don't you ever apologize for defending yourself." He brought his mouth to hers, sucking her lower lip, grazing it gently with his fangs. She kissed him back, now fully aroused. He looked so intimidating and dangerous in his Imperial attire, and she loved it. She'd scored herself a delicious Prince from an evil empire and she didn't want to share him with anyone. "I'm sorry you had to go through that. I didn't think Alerak would be so stupid as to come in here."

Sera yelped as Xal scooped her up into his arms, lifting her effortlessly. "You know," he rumbled, "it turns me on."

"What?" Sera curled against him, enjoying the way he held her close, inhaling his spicy, masculine scent. His body was warm and solid, his arms like corded steel.

"The fact that my female can kick ass when she's cornered. The thought makes me hard."

"Oh, you like that do you, big boy?" Sera basked in his praise, a warm feeling settling in her belly. Xal looked down at her, his eyes full of wonder.

"What made you learn to fight?" Curious, he inclined his head. Sera took a deep breath, leaning into him.

"You've seen my scars," she murmured, meeting his gaze. The clouds of anger had disappeared, leaving his golden eyes clear. He was focused only on her. Sera sighed. "When I was a kid, I was in this horrible accident. My father was on a diplomatic mission to a small planet called Xaron-3. I was sent to visit him on my school break, but the transporter I was on ran into an asteroid belt and took damage. When they tried to land on Xaron-3, it crashed. Everyone died except me. I felt I should have died that day, Xal. I had the worst case of survivor's remorse."

"I'm sorry." He planted another soft kiss on her forehead.

"They didn't have proper medical facilities on that planet. When I got back to Earth, I was an absolute mess. I should have lost my arm and half my face, but my father brought in the best specialists from all over the world. The me you see today is the result of years of painful treatment. They told me I would never use my arm again, but then my father volunteered me for a medical trial. They re-grew the muscle and bone from stem cells."

"Obviously you didn't let it hold you back."

"It was hard at first. I was hideous. Half of me was constantly wrapped up in dressings. I was teased. They called me 'monster'. That's hard for a kid to take, Xal. Even my own family started treating me differently."

"They had no right to treat you that way."

"Just like Kordolians, Humans can be cruel. I was angry. I withdrew into myself. I hated everything and everyone. And then one day, one of my physical therapists showed me how to use a speedball. It's basically a punching bag. And suddenly, I was able to release all of that anger. I was hooked. I joined a gym. I trained hard. My body healed and my arm and shoulder became strong. In the ring, I started kicking some serious ass. I became the monster they made me out to be, and it felt good."

"A beautiful monster," Xal whispered teasingly, sucking on her earlobe. "My monster."

Sera laughed. "They stopped calling me that a long time ago. These days, it's 'queen bitch'. And only ever behind my back."

"You are strong, my Queen." Xal moved across the room and lay her down on the bed, climbing on top of her. "Much stronger than I am. I won't let anyone say otherwise. Remind me to call in on your family when we return to Earth. If they cause you problems, I will deal with them."

"Don't worry about them. We've reached an uneasy truce," Sera murmured, although a part of her would love to see her father's face when Xal walked through the door. And her mother would probably have a heart attack.

She smirked at the thought as she fumbled with the fastenings of his jacket. Xal stilled her hands and ran a finger down the closure. It miraculously unzipped, and he shrugged the garment off. Underneath, he wore a light black shirt with a deep vee at the neck. It revealed the broad muscles of his chest, which gleamed and flexed as he prowled over her, watching her with hungry eyes.

"I must apologize for my treatment of you earlier," he rumbled, and a thrill coursed through her. She wanted him so badly. "I will make it up to you."

"Yes, Master," she said pretend-meekly, but she was smiling.

Xal skillfully undressed her, his hands exploring her body with a light caress that became reverent when he touched her scars. "Now that I know of the pain behind these," he whispered, "they are even more precious to me."

He said the damnedest things, that made her feel all warm and fuzzy inside. Sera fiddled with the opening of his pants. "Why are Kordolian garments so complicated?" she complained. "You're still in an inappropriate state of, uh, being dressed."

Xal inclined his head and tore off his shirt, revealing his impressive torso. Sera stared unashamedly at the defined ridges of his pecs and abdominal muscles. She wanted to lick him all over and devour him.

He was silver, alien perfection.

Xal noticed the direction of her gaze and grinned. His smile was adorable. It transformed his face, making him look cute and boyish, only with fangs. "There's more where that came from." He unbuckled his belt and threw his sword across the floor. It landed with a dull clatter as he pulled down his trousers, his huge length springing forth.

Moisture glistened at the tip of his cock. Sera pulled him forward, bringing him towards her. He knelt over her, straddling her and she placed her lips on him, tasting his wetness.

Xal moaned as she took him inside her mouth, moving back and forth along his hard shaft. His low, guttural moans surrounded her, and he twined his fingers through her hair, his caress soft and tender.

She sucked him and he voiced his appreciation, the sound of his pleasure washing over her and stoking her own arousal. He let her take her time as she savored the taste of him; the feel of him, running her fingers up his strong, muscular thighs.

Then he drew himself out gently, bringing her forward, and in a single, agile movement, they had reversed positions, and she was on top of him. He lay flat on his back, looking up at her, his pale, silky hair arranged around him in an abstract halo.

He was otherworldly and impossible and she took a moment to marvel at how such a being had become hers. The wildness she had sensed in him brimmed to the surface as he watched her with eyes of swirling gold.

"I'm all yours," Xal said as she moved over him. He pulled her close and then he was inside her, filling her completely, and Sera cried out with the sheer ecstasy of it as she started to grind her hips.

Xal smiled, content to watch her as a primal rhythm overtook her and she moved faster, her strong, lithe body swaying back and forth.

Sera gripped both of his horns as she fucked him, and Xal closed his eyes, a raw sound issuing from deep within his throat. His hands curved around her ass, guiding her, his movements strong yet gentle. His fingers traveled up her back, tracing its defined contours, reaching the part over her left shoulder where the scars began.

She fucked him slow, hard and deep, and his hands moved over her breasts, his nimble fingers caressing her nipples.

As her rhythm started to become more frenzied and her grip on his horns tightened, he sat up, bringing Sera's legs around him as she leaned into him.

A wild spirit had overtaken her, and she moved even faster as he wrapped her in his powerful, warm embrace, his voice blending with hers as they moaned and sighed. Sera was driven by the feel of him inside her; every time she thrust downwards along the length of him the ridges along his cock grazed her clit, sending her into a spiral of erotic bliss.

There was an exquisite tightness in her core that increased the faster she moved, and as the intensity of their lovemaking grew, that sensation built, and she was helpless to it, her body moving of its own accord.

Now Xal took over, placing his hands behind her and easing her down onto her back as he started to move, pumping his hips, gasping as he slammed his body against hers, his movements becoming rough and savage.

She growled as he placed his hands on her hips and fucked her harder, again and again until her legs became like jelly and all she knew was that she was going to come.

He was the perfect combination of brutality and gentleness.

She was overwhelmed with the sheer force of him as he plunged himself into her, again and again.

She was drowning in pleasure.

When he started to go even faster, she knew he was going to bring them the release they both craved.

His strong hands wrapped around the back of her neck. She moved her hands up and down his muscular back. Heat radiated from him, and she was slick with sweat. He brought his head up, closing his eyes again, arcing his back as he slammed into her.

Again and again.

He moaned her name, as if it were honey on his lips.

And then he came.

Sera's soft grunts became louder and higher, and in a moment she was going to scream as the beginnings of an orgasm started to ripple through her, becoming waves of intense pleasure.

The climax ripped through her like lightning, and as she screamed, Xal pulled her into him, her cries muffled as she buried her face in the crook of his shoulder.

He held her as the tension drained from her body and the most fantastic afterglow started to seep through her.

His arms were around her. He smelled so good. She wished they could stay like that forever.

But there were enemies to defeat and escapes to plot. Stark reality returned to her like a slap in the face. As long as they were on this ship, she was in mortal danger.

How long could Xal keep up the facade?

"I've made up my mind," he said, as he withdrew from her, rolling onto his side and curling his long limbs protectively around her. "We're not going to the Fleet Station. We're going to escape, and then I'm going to tell Tarak to blast the shit out of them. They won't know what hit them."

"Didn't you all want to avoid a firefight to minimize collateral damage?"

He put a finger against her lips. "You took a risk by coming with me. You almost got hurt by Alerak. That's all I can tolerate. I'm pulling you out of here. We've traveled far enough that Earth is out of *Ristval V's* firing range now. *Silence* will do the rest."

He kissed her gently on the top of her head, stroking her hair. "You've done your part, my crazy, brave female. We will leave the rest up to the former Imperial Military. And don't worry. Earth is no longer in the crossfire."

———

XAL LEFT her sprawled naked in his sleeping pod, stealing one last look at her toned, sinuous body. He hated to leave her, even for a short period of time, but he had to make contact with Tarak.

He had left her his Callidum sword, just in case Alerak returned.

The Qualum door obviously wasn't as secure as he'd thought.

He headed back towards the docking bay, where their transport was parked. The large, cavernous space was occupied by sleek fighter craft, their black Callidum hulls glinting ominously in the faint light.

The guards stood to attention as he passed.

"Where is my transport?" Xal demanded, pinning one of the soldiers with a harsh glare.

"I'm sorry, Prince Kazharan, but you aren't authorized to be here. General's orders."

Xal stepped close to the guard, towering over him. "I need to retrieve something important to me, soldier. Are you saying you won't let me pass?" Xal took a quick inventory of the soldiers blocking his way. There were three of them, and they all had plasma guns. He had nothing except his title. "I outrank Daegan, soldier," he said mildly. "Your insubordination may cause all kinds of trouble for you when you return to the Empire."

The guard paled. Most Kordolians didn't know of the crime Xal had committed against the Empress. They didn't know he had gone into exile. All this soldier knew was that Xal was a Prince of the Empire; Empress Vionn's own flesh and blood, and by extension, his word was absolute.

Xal hated throwing his weight around like this, but it had to be done.

The soldiers bowed and let him pass, and Xal ducked into the transport, pulling the door shut behind him. He hit the communication panel, sending a direct signal through to *Silence*.

"Xalikian." Tarak appeared instantly, his red eyes alert and questioning. "All goes to plan?"

"Somewhat. There was an incident involving my Human. I don't know how much longer I'll be able to keep up the act. Soon, they will grow suspicious."

"You didn't kill anyone, did you?" The General's voice was dry, but Xal got the impression he was amused.

"Not yet," Xal replied. "Although I might soon, if we don't get off this ship. There's enough distance between us and Earth now. They cannot attack Earth from here. I've identified some escape pods. I'm going to get Sera and eject. You should be able to track me through my implant and organize a retrieval."

"Yes. The sheer velocity of the escape pods can make them difficult to track, but I will find you."

"I'm sorry we weren't able to last longer. This has proven to be more difficult than I anticipated."

"That's because you are compromised."

"What?"

"It's obvious you've mated with your Human, and now you would crush anything and anyone that tries to harm her."

Xal gaped. "Is it that obvious?" As the General's words sank in, Xal realized he spoke the truth.

Tarak shrugged. "It happens. Objectivity dies, but you gain something greater. Trust me; I know the feeling."

"And what about *Ristval V*?"

"I had a feeling this might happen, so we're coming after it. We now have the advantage of surprise." He bared his fangs. "I'm not sure Daegan's ever been in a direct firefight in space."

He left the obvious unspoken. Xal wondered how many hostile engagements Tarak would have been in during his career. Hundreds? Thousands?

"You've done what you set out to do, my Prince. Earth is in the clear. Now, allow me to take over. I've been wanting to destroy these fuckers ever since they appeared in our sights. The only thing stopping me was the threat to Earth. It will take us approximately one phase to catch up to them. Then, we attack. Make sure you and your female are well clear by then."

"Yes, Sir," Xal said ironically, a wave of urgency taking hold of him. They had to get out of there soon, because all hell was about to break loose.

CHAPTER FIFTEEN

Xal entered his chambers and found them empty. There were signs of a recent struggle. The sheets of his sleeping pod were in disarray, and his Callidum blade was discarded on the floor.

He swore dirtily and heavily in Kordolian.

Anger like he'd never known before flooded through him.

This must have been Alerak's doing. The stupid, pompous little Councilor didn't know when to stop. With rage pumping in his veins, he stepped out into the corridor and started to run, sword in hand.

Where would they take her?

The holding cells, perhaps?

He came across a guard in the corridor and before the soldier knew what was happening, Xal was on top of him, disabling him with a blow to the head, kicking his feet out from under him and bringing him to the floor.

Xal had never encountered real live combat in his life, but he had spent hundreds upon thousands of phases hunting in the wild, sparring with his brothers, the Aikun, and fighting in the training room onboard *Silence*. He had killed monsters these Kordolians were no match for with his bare hands.

Physically, he had a supreme advantage.

He pulled the soldier's plasma gun from its holster and held it to his head. "Where did they take my Human?"

The soldier froze, unable to comprehend what was happening. Xal ground the point of the gun further into his temple. "I am this close to killing you, soldier. Tell me what I need to know."

The soldier raised a shaky arm, pointing towards a juncture. "They went that way."

"And where does that corridor lead, soldier?"

"M-medical bay."

Xal released him and ran, keeping the plasma gun. He followed the corridor downwards and realized that the layout of the ship mirrored *Silence*. He ran so fast that the few guards he passed stared after him in blank confusion, probably shocked at the sight of the Imperial Prince barreling down the corridors.

He ran straight to the medical bay, where the entrance was open. Voices floated to him from inside.

"That's not Akkadian's Human."

"What are you talking about, Mirkel?"

"I examined that Human when I was working on *Silence*. This one has different coloring and different hair. And the other one didn't have those strange scars and markings."

There was a pause as the information took time to sink in. "Kazharan has tricked us?" Alerak gasped, as Xal appeared before them. The Councilor was conversing with another Kordolian Xal didn't recognize; this male was tall and thin and had a cybernetic prosthesis attached to his right arm in the place where his hand was supposed to be. He wore the white robes of a medic.

They spun as Xal entered the room with his plasma gun raised. The Callidum sword was in his other hand. He aimed his gun at Alerak. "Where is she?"

"Summon the guards," Alerak shouted. "Alert General Daegan!" He looked up in panic at a glowing holoscreen. "The

Prince has betrayed us." He stared at Xal with venom in his pale yellow eyes.

Xal stalked forward, bringing the point of his blade up, pressing it against Alerak's throat. "Where. Is. She?"

"Put that down, Kazharan," he spluttered.

"Don't give me bad news, Alerak." Xal applied a little more pressure, the sword breaking the delicate skin of Alerak's neck. "I don't think I can cope with bad news right now."

Xal sensed movement behind him. A quick flick of his eyes told him the medic was approaching with a sedative in hand. Xal pointed the plasma gun and fired, the bright blue bolt just missing the medic as he dived for cover. The recoil reverberated through his arm, but he held steady. These things had quite the kick. It was his first time using such a weapon. There was a loud explosion as the black wall behind them absorbed its impact.

"Don't move," he growled. "The next one has your face written on it, medic."

"You will regret this, Prince. Your mother won't tolerate—"

Xal drew blood. A trickle of black blood ran down Alerak's neck, staining the orange fabric of his robes. "I don't want to hear about my mother, Alerak. Where is the Human?"

"You're insane."

"I am. And there's no telling what a crazy person might do. Impaling you crosses my mind." Xal lost patience and slashed Alerak's cheek. The councilor gasped in shock, bringing his hand up to the cut. Black blood seeped through his fingers.

"Just testing," Xal shrugged. "The next one is for your neck."

"She's in the examination room," Alerak blurted.

"If she's been harmed in any way, you will learn the true meaning of the word 'suffering'." Xal slowly brought his sword down, daring Alerak to try anything. But Nobles weren't fighters, and the Councilor was too petrified to move against him.

Behind him, the medic moved again, raising some kind of

projectile firing device, probably a tranq dart gun. Xal spun
and fired his weapon. The medic was thrown back into the
wall, a gaping wound in his chest. "I told you not to move." He
didn't care if the medic lived or died. His only priority was to
find Sera. If they had done anything to her, there was going to
be a bloodbath.

There was no need to pretend whose side he was on
anymore.

"You killed him!" Alerak recoiled in horror.

"What did you expect, Councilor?" He bared his fangs.
"You kill your slaves. Mother kills her subjects. I simply kill
those who take what is mine. It's the Kordolian way. And if she
is harmed, you're dead too. The only reason I'm not sending
you to one of Kaiin's hells right now is that I have a little task
for you. Move, Luron." He pointed the gun at him.

"You are mad," Alerak gasped in horror.

"Probably," Xal said mildly, as they entered the examination room. He stopped dead in his tracks.

Sera was laid out on an examination table, naked and
sedated. Tiny, red-pointed needles had been inserted at
various points all over her body. They were present in her
ankles, knees, wrists and shoulders.

He had thought he was angry before. Now, the rage
pumping through his veins turned to ice.

"What have you done to her, Alerak?" he asked softly, as
he reached her side. Alerak made a sudden movement, trying
to bolt for the exit.

"Guards!" he screamed.

Several Kordolian soldiers appeared, their weapons
pointed at Xal.

"I-immobilize him," Alerak ordered. "But whatever you do,
don't kill him. The Infinite Mother wants him alive. If he dies,
we all die."

The soldiers advanced slowly, watching Xal cautiously.

"Take another step and I'll shoot Councilor Alerak," Xal

warned. "Your move, Luron. Do they keep coming, or do they leave?" He raised the gun. "You want to end up like the medic?"

"Retreat!" Alerak yelled. The soldiers froze. Xal waved the point of his weapon threateningly. Alerak's eyes widened. "Move! This is an Imperial order!"

They disappeared.

Alerak held up his hands. "We haven't done anything to it," he stuttered. "I was going to ask Mirkel to do a little capacity reduction surgery, that's all. This slave is too strong. You saw how it attacked me. Those are just tendon and nerve markers. They can be easily removed. It has not yet been harmed. Look at the monitor. It breathes. Its heart beats. It is merely sedated." He took a step backwards. "This is all a misunderstanding, Prince Kazharan. A safety measure, for your sake. Your slave would have been returned to you."

Xal whirled and stalked towards Alerak with death in his eyes. He held the Callidum sword at his side, keeping the plasma gun pointed at the Councilor. Alerak retreated until his back was pressed against the wall.

Alerak's breath came in deep, shaky gasps. Confusion swirled in his pale eyes. "Why are you doing this, Kazharan?"

Xal pressed the gun against his chest. "I just had a vision," he said slowly, his voice as frigid and bleak as the glacial plains of Kythia's windswept Vaal. "I'll tell you a little something about where that vision came from." He came up close, so the words he spoke were just a little louder than a deathly whisper. "I had a twin brother," he hissed, digging the tip of the gun into Alerak's bony flesh. "His name was Amun, and he was destined to rule the Empire. He was stronger and cleverer than me, and he always protected me." Xal plunged his sword into Alerak's foot. The Councilor screamed. "I'll let that rest there for a while."

"You're crazy," Alerak said, his voice hoarse.

"I haven't finished," Xal snapped. He grabbed Alerak's

face, the sharp points of his obsidian nails digging into Alerak's skin. "Now mother began to disagree with father about who should succeed the throne. For some reason, she thought I would be easier to manipulate than Amun. Their fights became more and more vicious, until one day, father had enough. You know, I remember the way you looked back then, Alerak. I remember the expressions on the twelve faces of the High Councillors as Amun and I stood before you, and father declared that we were to be sent to the Vaal, defenseless and on our own, for one whole cycle. Whoever survived was to ascend the throne."

"I did not—"

"You all voted in favor of it, Alerak. Don't take me for a fool. The entire idea would have appealed to your warped Kordolian sense of narcissism. The strongest wins; that's what you think. You must have known by then that Emperor Ilhan had been insane since his consciousness was transferred into that new body of his." Xal's hand trembled with barely restrained rage. "But still, you let Amun and I go out into the Vaal with nothing more than the clothes on our backs. Two children, sent to survive in the wild. What did you expect would happen? A *Szkazajik* came upon us. Amun tried to fend it off; he told me to run. We attacked it with our tiny claws and fangs, but we were only children. I had to watch as it ran away with my brother's broken, dead body in its mouth. That's when the Aikun found me. They took me in and raised me for six cycles, until I returned to the Palace. Apparently, I was the worthy successor." Bitterness crept into Xal's tone. Alerak was frozen, almost afraid to breathe.

"The same stupidity that caused the death of my brother later led to the death of my only child, all because of some idiotic prophecy," he spat. "So two very precious individuals have been taken from me in my lifetime, Councilor, and this Human female just so happens to be precious to me." He lifted the sword out of Alerak's foot. The Councilor gasped in agony.

Xal stamped down on his foot, grinding into it. Alerak screamed. "So you can understand if I go a little 'insane' when you take what belongs to me. The Aikun have a tradition they reserve for their most hated enemies. It involves carving the beating heart out of one's chest. *That* was the vision I had, Alerak. That is what I want to do to you right now." Xal lifted his sword and stabbed it into Alerak's right shoulder, pinning him to the wall. Alerak cried out in pain, staring at Xal in absolute terror. But there was also a glimmer of adoration in his eyes.

Some small, sick part of Alerak was loving what Xal was doing to him. Xal turned away in disgust.

"But I won't do that, Councilor, because I want you to return with a message for mother. You tell her that Earth is *mine*, and that the prophecy she feared so much is about to come true. The Empire is dying, Alerak, but we are going to survive."

He left his father's sword inside Alerak, who was whimpering in pain, pinned to the wall and unable to move for fear of being cut by an impossibly sharp Callidum blade.

As Xal turned towards Sera, he froze, meeting her wide-eyed brown gaze.

She was awake.

PAIN WAS no stranger to Sera, but those weird little needles that creepy Kordolian doctor had stuck in her really fucking hurt.

That was her first thought as the sedative wore off.

Her second thought was that Xal sounded really, really angry. Scary angry. His voice was so cold she thought the air might freeze. She had never been so glad to see him. Relief flooded through her.

Sera tried to move, but she couldn't. The little needles seemed to have paralyzed her.

She could, however, turn her head. Amazingly, they hadn't discovered the little translating device that sat in her ear. Her wild hair had hidden it nicely.

She watched as Xal pinned Alerak to the wall, plunging the sword into his right shoulder. Through a fog of pain, she had heard everything Xal said.

Lying naked on that cold, clinical table, it struck her.

He was afraid of losing her.

The realization washed away the pain, turning it into a dull, bearable ache. And she found that she didn't recoil in fear when Xal turned to her, his hand stained with Alerak's black blood, even though his expression was terrifying.

He was enraged, but as he looked at her, his elegant features softened, and he rushed to her side. He swore in Kordolian, and some of the translated words made her blush.

Xal wiped his bloodied hand on his jacket and started removing the needles. It hurt, but Sera felt movement returning to her limbs.

He worked quickly, his long fingers pulling those awful needles out of her body with great tenderness, despite the speed of his movements.

"I'm sorry, Xal," she said, as she started to shiver. The metal table she lay on was damn cold.

His eyes widened in shock, the anger starting to drain from his face. "Whatever for?"

"I didn't realize how difficult it was for you to allow me to come with you."

"Don't be sorry. You had a point about Humans and Kordolians working together. And we achieved what we set out to do. Earth is outside *Ristval V's* firing range now." He lifted her left hand and kissed it, before moving down to remove the pins from her legs. Small, red puncture wounds remained, but Sera was now able to move freely. She sat up as Xal removed the last of the needles, tossing them on the floor.

"Can you walk?" Tenderly, he lifted her off the table and set her on her feet.

"No problem." Sera's legs hurt like hell, but a little pain wasn't going to stop her.

"Can you run?"

"You bet I can." After being freed from that needle-torture, she felt like she could run a marathon. Sera rubbed her arms, gooseflesh rising on them. She was still naked.

"Here." Xal peeled off his black jacket and draped it across her shoulders. She slid her arms into the sleeves, grateful for its warmth. He slid his finger down the front and the closure came together. It was huge on her, coming to about mid-thigh, and it carried his crisp, masculine scent.

Sera looked around for her leggings, but they were gone. It didn't matter. Xal's long jacket covered all the important bits.

"We need to get out of here now," he said, taking her by the hand. As they passed Alerak, Xal stopped, and pulled the black sword out of the wall, and out of Alerak. The Councilor gasped in shock and crumpled to the floor, putting a hand over the wound in his shoulder.

"You fucking stabbed me," Alerak cried, as Xal motioned for him to get up.

"Yes," Xal agreed. "I did. Come now, you'll be our hostage. If anyone tries to attack us, you die." He brought the tip of the blade underneath Alerak's chin and made him stand. The Councilor grunted in pain.

Sera looked across the room and saw a wad of gauze type things on a metal table laden with surgical instruments. She shuddered. Those things had been meant for her.

She picked up the gauze and held it out to Alerak. "Press this against your shoulder," she said in Universal. "It will stop the bleeding."

The Kordolian stared back at her in shock. Xal raised both eyebrows.

She shrugged. "I feel a bit sorry for him."

"After what he did to you?"

"He's an asshole, but I'll bet that wound hurts like a bitch."

Xal shook his head in disbelief. Alerak pressed the wad to his shoulder and started to walk. Xal held the plasma gun to Alerak's head, the sword in his other hand. "Remember, any stupidity and your head gets blown off. No-one is to attack us. Are you clear, Alerak?"

"Y-yes."

"We may have to run, Sera."

"I'm ready." She winced as she flexed her arms. "Let's get out of this madhouse before they decide to turn me into a pincushion again."

CHAPTER SIXTEEN

As they made their way down the corridors, heading towards the docking bay, Xal ordered Alerak to walk in front of them, his plasma gun pressed into the Councilor's back. They made an odd procession; the limping Alerak, Xal in the middle with the gun and finally Sera following close behind.

Every time the guards appeared, Alerak fearfully ordered them back and they obeyed without hesitation. Wounded and disheveled he might be, but he was still a High Councilor; a Kordolian from a distinguished Noble House. On Kythia, his life was apparently worth something.

Xal regarded the whole situation with a certain sense of satisfaction. Alerak was a most effective hostage.

They stepped across the threshold into the cavernous docking bay and Xal wasn't surprised to see General Daegan standing on the walkway above them. Stationed on either side of him were soldiers with guns.

"Xalikian." Daegan's deep voice echoed throughout the space. "What do you think you're doing?"

"We're leaving, Daegan," Xal replied. "Don't try to stop us."

"I'm giving you one last chance to re-consider, Prince.

Think of what your actions mean for our people and for the Empire. You would intentionally destroy our race by tainting your offspring with Human blood?"

"The Empire will be gone in one generation, Daegan." Xal stared back at the General. Daegan appeared awkward standing amongst his soldiers. His uniform was ill-fitted, the fabric straining around his generous waist. His expression was resigned. "So why are you still fighting?"

Daegan shook his head. "We will find a way to survive," he said, but there was no conviction in his voice. "Your mother needs you, Xalikian."

"Vionn lost me when she killed my child, Daegan. What did you expect would happen?"

"That child was a danger to the Empire, Xalikian. It was written in the prophecies. Your mother did it to save us. She hopes that with time, you will understand."

Xal took a deep breath, trying to hold back the tide of anger that threatened to overwhelm him. He couldn't afford to let rage overcome him now. Not when Sera was beside him, wounded and in pain, and they had a clear path to their escape route.

He pushed Alerak in front of him, so that the Councilor was in the firing line. Black blood dotted the polished floor, dripping from Alerak's wound. He swayed on his feet as Xal shot Sera a quick glance. "Get ready to run," he mouthed.

He raised the plasma gun and looked Daegan in the eye. "I don't believe in prophecies," he snarled, and fired.

The blue bolt shot just wide of Daegan and his troops, who ducked for cover. Xal pushed Alerak away and looked at Sera.

"Run!"

And they did just that.

SERA RAN FASTER than she ever had before. Xal went off like a bullet, dashing across the floor of the docking bay with Sera close behind. She pushed through the pain caused by a hundred needle-inflicted injuries and went after him, pumping her arms and legs.

She was thankful that she'd worked hard to keep herself physically fit. All her training was now paying off.

A hail of plasma-fire followed them, shaking the floor, deafening booms reverberating through the space. Xal ducked behind a fighter and they were momentarily shielded from the blasts.

"There's an escape room down that passageway," he whispered, pointing into the shadows. There was indeed an exit there. Sera could just barely make it out in the dim light.

A plasma bolt grazed the tail of the fighter, sending out a shower of sparks. Sera yelped as Xal scooped her up into his arms and ran, hunching his large body protectively over her.

He sped down the corridor with powerful strides until they reached a dark, circular room. It was lined with strange black capsules that were distinctly person-sized.

As they entered the room, there was a loud whoosh, and the capsules started disappearing, sucked down into some mysterious, hidden void below.

Xal swore profusely and ran towards the last remaining capsule, slamming his hand on a panel. Its door slid open, revealing a pod-like space that was clearly designed to fit a single person.

"They've ejected the other escape pods," Xal growled, looking around the room in desperation. "Fucking Daegan. I caught this one just in time. As long as the door's open, the eject mechanism is overridden."

As he looked at Sera, his expression lost all its fierceness. "Get in," he said softly.

He wanted her to get inside the last pod.

Sera met his molten gaze and felt a huge, gaping hole open

up inside of her. Her mouth opened wide, and she uttered a soundless "*no*".

"Get in, Sera." Xal's tone brooked no argument.

She shook her head. "What about you?"

"I'll figure something out," he said gently, leaving the obvious unspoken. He might not be joining her. Ever.

Sera clenched her fists, and for the first time in years, tears started to brim in her eyes. "I'm not going anywhere without you, Xalikian. We can both squeeze inside that thing."

"No, Sera. The oxygen wouldn't be enough for both of us. You need to go."

"I'm not leaving without you." He started to bundle her up and place her inside the pod. Sera fought against him like a wildcat, but his muscular arms were like steel. She managed to get an arm free. Sera slapped him in the face.

Speechless, Xal blinked.

"You stupid, big, silver idiot," she snapped. "What will it take to knock some sense into you? You're not just going to bundle me into this little pod and shoot me off into space. There has to be a way. Don't be so quick to sacrifice yourself, Xal. Don't you understand that I need you?"

His mouth was wide open in shock, revealing his fangs.

Sera scanned the room, looking for something; anything. "What are those things?" She pointed to a rack on the wall. Several black armor-looking things hung from the wall. They looked like big robotic exoskeletons.

"Maintenance suits, I think." A glimmer of an idea appeared in Xal's eyes. He leaned in and kissed her, managing to look a little sheepish. "I was perhaps, a little hasty. Hold on..." He handed her the sword and the plasma gun. "Keep your foot in the pod. Don't let the door close under any circumstances. Wait here."

Xal walked over to the rack and inspected one of the suits. It had a large black faceless helmet and it was made entirely of metal. There was a pack of some sort attached to its back, with what looked like an oxygen concentrator and various robotic tools. A claw-like hook was also attached to the pack.

As Xal pressed a panel on its chest, it came to life, blue lights flickering across the visor. "Its oxygen won't last as long as the pod's, but it gives me a chance."

He returned to where Sera stood. Voices reached them from down the corridor. He knelt down beside her and gestured towards his sword. "I need you to trim my horns," he said. "Evolution didn't factor the wearing of helmets into its grand plan. Quickly, Sera."

Sera looked at Xal's gracefully curved horns, and then at the sword in her hand. Despite its menacing appearance, the black blade was surprisingly light. She hesitated. She loved his horns. They gave him such intense sexual pleasure.

"It's all right, my love," Xal reassured her. "They'll grow back."

Sera shook her head, admiring Xal's beautiful horns for the last time before she brought down the sword. The black blade sliced through the first one like butter, and Xal gasped in pain, his features twisting. Sera's hands trembled. She struggled with the idea that she was causing him such pain.

"Cut the other one," Xal snarled, through gritted teeth.

Sera chopped off his remaining horn. Xal cried out and swore profusely. A thin trickle of black blood trailed down his temples and cheeks from where the horns had been severed.

The harsh shouts of the Kordolian soldiers were becoming louder now. Xal rushed across and activated the exo-suit. The metal body opened, and he stepped in front of it, turning his back.

He spoke a command in Kordolian, and then the whole thing started to wrap around him, enclosing his body with metal. The visor concealed his features, but he reassured Sera with a wave of his hand.

He froze for a moment, appearing to get himself acquainted with the suit and its controls. The various implements and objects on it moved, and one clattered to the floor. It seemed he didn't really know how to operate the suit.

In frustration, Xal pulled at the hook-thing attached to the pack with his metal-gloved hands, and it came out, a long, black, metallic line attached to it.

Xal rushed across to Sera as Kordolian soldiers started to fill the room, their guns raised. Before she could protest, he had lifted her up and shoved her inside the pod. The Kordolian soldiers started to fire. Xal shielded her with his armored body. He grabbed the hook-thing and slammed it into the body of the pod, its metal claws digging firmly into the black metal. The line attached to it was connected to Xal's exo-suit.

Sera stared at him as he gave her a single nod. Then, he slammed the door of the pod shut and crossed his arms across his chest.

There was a great *whoosh*, and everything turned to black.

CHAPTER SEVENTEEN

The pod was tight and dark, and Sera held her breath as the force of the sudden, massive acceleration ripped through her body, pinning her against the padded surface. Pain shot through her as her limbs were compressed, and she closed her eyes, fighting the terror and panic that threatened to overwhelm her.

Then, the acceleration stopped, the pressure lessened, and they were in space, shooting past the stars at impossible speed. There was a small, clear panel in the pod that allowed her to see the dark body of the *Ristval V* disappearing behind them.

A few lazy plasma shots were fired after them, but they were already too far away and too small for any of them to hit. In any case, *Ristval V* didn't have time to be going after the small fry. A larger distraction loomed. Sera saw the now-familiar outline of the warship *Silence* zeroing in on *Ristval V* like a big hungry black shark.

There was going to be a firefight.

Frantically, she peered down through the window and saw Xal's suited figure trailing after her, attached to the short, metal line he had managed to hook onto the pod's surface just before they were ejected.

With no opposing forces to slow them or hold them back, they continued on at the same impossible speed, traveling further into nothingness.

There was nothing out here, save for the backdrop of stars and the inky blackness of outer space.

Despite the insulated interior it was cold inside the pod, and Sera shivered, thankful for Xal's thick jacket. His scent surrounded her, and she stared outside, watching him with a sense of rising dread.

He looked so small and vulnerable against the backdrop of space.

He'd put her safety ahead of his.

The big idiot had even been willing to stay behind, just so she could escape.

Sera shook her head in frustration. That stupid, stubborn, sweet Kordolian male.

It had to be beyond freezing out there. How much insulation did that metal exo-suit of his have? And how much oxygen did he have to go on?

Sera wished there was some way to communicate with him. Had he even survived the ejection process?

She had no way of knowing.

All she could do was watch him and hope there was life inside that dark, faceless suit.

They'd hit inertia now, moving at a constant speed, which was still impossibly fast. But without the acceleration, Sera felt weightless. Only the walls of the pod were holding her in place. It was obviously designed for someone much bigger, because she had a fair bit of room to move around.

She wished there was something she could do, dammit! But for the first time in a long time, she found herself completely helpless; powerless.

All she could do was wait, and hope to hell that Tarak and his crew found them soon.

To her intense relief, Xal started to move. He grabbed the

line attaching his suit to the pod and started to pull himself towards her, one hand at a time. Eventually, he reached the pod and somehow managed to latch onto it, digging in with his metal-gloved hands.

Staring out, Sera put her hand against the window. Xal peered inside and placed his hand against the glass, over hers.

"Sera." His warm voice filled the pod, startling her. "I finally figured out how to use the comm inside this infernal thing. Are you okay?"

"I'm fine." She shuddered in relief. He was alive and talking to her, and the sound of his voice was the greatest thing in the Universe right now. "You?"

"Battered. Fucking sore. But alive."

"What happens now?"

"We wait. Tarak will come for us. It might take a while, but he'll come. Just sit still now. Don't move. After this, I won't talk anymore. Let's conserve our oxygen. Try to get some sleep."

"Okay." Sera looked at the smooth dark visor of Xal's suit and wished she could see his face. She wanted to see his eyes; she wanted to see him smile. She yearned to feel the warmth of his silver skin against her own. She wanted his strong arms around her.

But they were separated by metal and glass and the weightless void of space.

On impulse, she pressed her lips against the glass, blowing him an imaginary kiss. She winked and forced a smile, even though a solitary tear had slipped down her cheek.

Shit. Was she crying?

Sera never cried. Most people on Earth thought she was a hard-as-nails bitch who wasn't capable of shedding tears. But here she was, stuck in the middle of space with beautiful, tortured Xal, hurtling unstoppably in some random direction.

Suck it up, girl.

It was hard enough for Xal already, being stuck on the

outside. She would not make things more difficult for him by letting him see her cry. So she took a deep breath, wiped away that single tear and settled in for the long wait.

She just hoped Xal's people caught up to them soon.

"SERA." Xal's voice was quiet, but Sera opened her eyes. She must have drifted off at some point. She rubbed her arms against the cold.

"Yes, Xal?"

"My oxygen's running low. I'm going to use a technique to slow my heartbeat. You won't hear from me again for a while, but don't worry. I'll be fine." The words were slow and softly murmured. Then, the line went quiet.

Sera banged her fist against the glass in frustration. Where the fuck was *Silence*? Where was the General?

Time was running out and there was nothing she could do.

She just had to hope against all hell that they would reach Xal in time.

And she prayed he could hold on, just a little bit longer.

CHAPTER EIGHTEEN

When she opened her eyes again, Sera wondered if she was dreaming. To their left was a sleek black cruiser, matching their speed. It was a small, fast craft, and it was obviously Kordolian, judging by its shape and the black metal of its hull.

Has the help finally arrived?

Xal was still latched onto the outside of her pod.

"Xal?" She didn't know if he could hear her.

There was no response.

"Xal!" Sera shouted. Still nothing. She banged her fist against the window of the escape pod, trying futilely to attract the attention of the cruiser, although she knew there was no way they could hear her.

It started to drift closer to them, maintaining its speed.

A long, flexible metal arm with a claw-like thing on one end began to extend from the cruiser.

It tried to grab onto them, but it wasn't long enough to reach them.

The cruiser maneuvered closer to them, the arm-thing wobbling about as it tried to latch onto her pod. It narrowly avoided Xal's motionless form and Sera drew in a sharp breath.

She sure as hell hoped these were the good guys, and she hoped beyond all hope that Xal was alive.

He'd said something about slowing down his heartbeat; using a technique of some kind. Perhaps he was in a trance-like state?

Please make it be that.

The alternative was too painful to think about.

Sera braced herself as the cruiser tried again, then again, to latch on. It wobbled and straightened and went for another attempt. To her intense relief, there was a metallic thud, and then they were moving, as the metal arm brought them towards the cruiser.

A hatch opened up on the side, and the arm drew them into an airlock.

As the hatch closed and the airlock depressurized, the cruiser's gravity kicked in, and the pod landed on the floor with a crash. It knocked Sera around, and she reflexively brought her arms above her head as she bumped into the padded surface of the pod.

Xal's metallic hands were still embedded in the surface of the pod, but he wasn't moving. Sera tried to push open the door, but it wouldn't budge.

She searched for a control panel, but she couldn't make anything out in the darkness.

"Hey!" she screamed. "Is anybody there!"

The other side of the airlock slid open, revealing Tarak and the female medic she'd seen on *Silence*. Sera almost sobbed in relief. She gestured towards Xal frantically. "Get him out of there first!"

Tarak wasted no time, pulling the exo-armor off the pod. He lay Xal's lifeless form gently on the floor and ripped his helmet off with his bare hands.

The medic opened the pod and Sera stumbled out, rushing over to Xal.

His eyes were closed and he wasn't moving. Sera put a

hand to his cheek. It was as cold as ice. His severed horns had bled, leaving trails of dried, black blood down both temples and cheeks. His appearance was surreal and terrifying. She didn't know whether he was dead or alive.

"Xal," she whispered, as the medic gently pulled her away.

Tarak pressed something and the rest of the exo-suit opened, revealing Xal's motionless body. Tarak placed a finger at his neck, checking for a pulse. The medic did the same, and they shared a knowing glance.

"He said something about a technique to try and slow down his heart," Sera said, her voice wavering. "He was running out of oxygen."

"Hm." Infuriatingly stoic as per usual, Tarak raised an eyebrow.

Sera was on the verge of flipping out. How could these two be so calm?

"Aren't you guys going to do something?" Sera's brain couldn't process the possibility that there was nothing more that could be done. She couldn't accept it. She reached up and felt wetness on her cheeks.

"He's not dead," Tarak said, and as Sera looked up she found stillness in his deep, red eyes. He wasn't worried at all. Slowly, the storm inside her mind and heart began to calm.

"What?"

"This is *anava*, a technique he learnt from the Aikun tribe." Tarak took her hand and placed it on Xal's chest, over his heart. "See."

Sera slipped her fingers under Xal's thin shirt, pressing against his bare skin, which was freezing. At first, she felt nothing. She looked up in alarm. Tarak and the medic gestured for her to remain still.

Then, she felt it.

Thud.

A single heartbeat, then nothing.

She waited. The silence stretched between them, impossibly long.

Thud.

There it was again. A heartbeat. They were so far apart; almost a minute or longer. His heart was beating extremely slowly.

"He's alive?" she whispered, hope soaring into her chest.

"Indeed."

Intense relief flooded through Sera. "And what the hell is this *anava* thing? How do we wake him up?"

"He's put himself into a deep trance." The medic regarded her with deep orange eyes that reminded her of a winter sunset on Nova Terra. "The Lost Tribes use *anava* to spend long periods of time underwater when they go hunting for sea creatures. That's what Xal's done, except he's gone way too deep this time."

"So how do we bring him out of this *anava*?"

"Heat." The medic shrugged. "I would put him in a hot room for several phases to replenish the energy that he's expelled. Bit by bit, his heart rate will increase, his vitals will come back to normal, and when they reach a certain threshold, he'll wake up."

"So he basically needs to get warm."

"That's right."

"Can you do that onboard this craft?"

"We don't have the facilities. This is just a stealth cruiser. We need to get him back to *Silence*."

Tarak frowned. "*Silence* is engaged in pursuit. It will be nearly impossible to catch them now."

A look of mild panic crossed the medic's face. "We can't delay. There is a small, but very real risk that his heart might stop altogether. The sooner we bring him out of it, the better."

Sera was on the verge of exploding. There was no way she was going to sit back and watch while Xal sank further into this eerie, trance-like state. "Where are we right now, General?" Worry and urgency bled into her voice. She put a hand on Xal's forehead, hoping vainly that some of her warmth would seep into him.

"You had drifted far. We are at an approximate midpoint between S*ilence* and Earth."

"There has to be something Human floating around here; something that would have decent facilities on board. Can you do a scan, General? We'll take anything; a mining station, cargo freighter, whatever. Put out a distress call."

"Hm." He got up and disappeared without another word.

The medic raised her eyebrows in concern. "Humans may be threatened by the sight of a Kordolian craft. Can you reassure them, Sera?"

"Oh, don't you worry about that," Sera growled, casting a protective glance over Xal. "I promise you, they will accommodate us if I have anything to do with it."

She touched the bare skin of his chest with her other hand. He was like an iceberg. It shook her to the core, but she buried her distress and fear deep inside. Now wasn't the time to fall apart. "I know you guys like the cold and all, but don't you have a thermo-wrap or some kind of blanket?"

The medic pushed the long tail of her lilac hair behind one shoulder and stood. "I'll see what I can do," she said softly, before giving Sera a long, appraising look.

She left Sera in the airlock with Xal, who barely breathed, and Sera wished she could wake her sleeping Prince with a kiss. He was so damn cold, and his features were glacial, as if they'd been carved from marble. How could life exist in this frozen body?

She'd just have to give him the only warmth she could find right now.

Hers.

UNDERNEATH THE BLANKET, Sera was naked, and so was Xal. She held onto him with growing desperation, pressing her body against his, hoping her heat would radiate into him and bring up his core temperature. She'd insisted on doing this, and to her surprise, neither of the Kordolians had thought twice about the naked Human curled around their Prince.

The medic, Zyara, had hooked him up to a transfusion of some kind of warmed fluid after they'd moved him to a small dock at the far end of the cruiser.

Still, he remained the same way, his heart beating at an impossibly slow pace, his body cold and still.

Sera pressed her ear to his chest, just to hear the reassuring *thud* of his heart. Zyara had attached him to a monitor, but Sera didn't understand the blips and data that flooded the holoscreen. It was all written in Kordolian, and their alphabet was like nothing she'd ever seen before.

So she relied on the rhythm of Xal's body to tell her that he was still alive.

She wanted nothing more than to feel his warm hands on her skin; to hear his soft, low voice whispering in her ear. She yearned for his touch, and until she heard his voice again, she wasn't letting him go.

Sera closed her eyes for a moment, trying to stem her tears. When she opened them again, Tarak was looming over her.

"There is a Human facility nearby," he said. "They are naturally reluctant to deal with Kordolians. I will give them one last chance to try and understand that if they do not co-operate, I will board them and start killing them one-by-one until they change their minds." He thrust a small communication device in front of her. "Talk to them. They may understand it better if they speak to one of their own kind."

"Oh, give that here," Sera snapped, yanking her arm out from under the blanket. "Hello?" She spoke into the smooth black device. The line crackled with patchy interference.

"I repeat, we will not allow non-Humans to board our

facility without official authorization. I'm sorry, but you're going to have to wait, or find another station that will accept your request." The voice that came across was definitely male, Human and bored-sounding.

"Excuse me," Sera snapped, "I understand you are refusing boarding rights because of security concerns, but we need urgent medical attention. I have an unwell crew member on board."

"Sorry ma'am, but I can't-"

Sera switched to English. "State your rank and the name of your facility, officer."

"Uh-" The officer paused, clearly surprised. "You're Human?"

"I am indeed Human, so will you please identify yourself?"

"Uh, you're speaking to Communications Officer Erikson, of the *MS Elvis*. May I request your name and credentials, ma'am, and may I ask, with all due respect, what the hell you're doing onboard a Kordolian stealth cruiser?"

Sera took a deep breath, closed her eyes and tried to center herself. This asshole was wasting time with stupid questions. "Officer Erikson, this is Sera Aquinas. I believe the corporation that owns your mining station is called GalaxyMetal. Am I correct?"

"Uh, yes, ma'am." Now he sounded bemused.

"And are you aware who the majority shareholders in GalaxyMetal are, Officer?"

"Last I heard, a big chunk had been acquired by the Aquinas family." Another pause. "Oh."

"Now I am requesting nicely that you allow our little cruiser to dock without any resistance, or you will be hearing from my lawyers. If you have any doubts, run a voiceprint ID on me. What happens in space gets dealt with on Earth, Officer, so if my father hears you denied me access in a time of need, you will be out of a job at the very least. Do you understand me, Erikson?"

For a moment, the line went completely silent, and Sera wondered if blind adherence to rules would prevail over common sense. She hated using her family's name to get her way, but this time, it couldn't be helped.

For the sake of the Humans onboard that mining station, she hoped they would do the right thing. She did not like the look on the General's face right now. His expression was really fucking scary.

The comm device crackled to life again. "Uh, my apologies for the delay, Miss Aquinas. We're opening Docking Bay One on portside, so you are cleared to proceed."

Sera handed the comm back to Tarak, who shrugged. "The Humans can consider themselves fortunate."

Under the blankets, Sera wrapped her body around Xal's, running her hands up and down his cold skin. She was freezing too, but she didn't care. She just wanted her Xal back.

And if any Human on the MS *Elvis* tried to get in the way, Jupiter help them, because between her and Tarak, she didn't know who would be more brutal.

CHAPTER NINETEEN

Sera jumped out of her tiny bunk as a jarring chime went off, yanking her from sleep. She ran a hand through her tousled hair, momentarily disoriented.

Then, it hit her.

They were on the *MS Elvis*, where they had stuck Xal in a tiny room with the heat cranked up to maximum, waiting for him to thaw out. After finding out exactly whose daughter Sera was, the Station Boss had been very accommodating, even though her guests were Kordolians. Zyara had been pretty confident that he would be fine, despite the extreme heat, and Sera had no choice but to trust the medic. At first, Sera had clung to Xal stubbornly, refusing to leave him until it had gotten so warm in there that she was at risk of getting heat stroke.

Exhausted, she'd reluctantly disentangled herself from Xal, with Zyara reassuring her that she would monitor him. So Sera had taken the time to have a very brief cold shower, jump into some standard-issue worker's scrubs and catch some shut-eye in a cramped capsule bed.

"What is it?" She hit the panel beside the door and it slid

open, revealing a very stressed-out looking pair of peace-keepers.

"I'm sorry to bother you Miss Aquinas, but your, uh, guest is awake."

"He is?" Sera almost punched the air in sheer joy. "How is he?"

"It's probably better for you to see for yourself." The peacekeepers were holding their bolt-rifles defensively and they still wore their combat helmets. They shared a mean-ingful glance.

Sera stiffened. "Is there a problem, officers?"

Please don't let there be a problem.

"The Kordolian is—"

"He's violent. Uncontrollable. Inhumanly fucking strong, excuse my language, ma'am. If he doesn't calm down we're going to have to escalate our use of force."

"You will do no such thing!" Sera slid her feet into a pair of slippers and pushed past the peacekeepers, breaking into a run despite their startled shouts. She sprinted down the corridor, with the peacekeepers struggling to catch up with her. She ran until she reached the small room where they had placed Xal.

Tarak had appeared at the other end of the corridor, with Zyara by his side. He strode towards them, glaring at the peace-keepers with the promise of death in his eyes. With his black, fitted exo-armor and grim expression, he was intimidating as hell.

"If you Humans have done anything to harm him..."

"He's already put three of us in the medical bay with broken bones!" One of the peacekeepers raised his bolt-cannon defensively. "All we've tried to do is restrain him!"

In the midst of a brewing storm, Sera held up her hand. "General Tarak," she said, trying to sound respectful, because he was the most dangerous of them all. "Please, just hang on for a moment."

She turned to the peacekeepers. "Lower your guns." At

first they hesitated. Sera glared at them and slowly, they complied.

Tarak inclined his head and for a split-second, Sera thought she saw a flicker of amusement cross his features. She shook her head. Whatever. Kordolians were strange.

"Zyara," she said slowly. "What is going on with our Prince?"

"He's very much awake," the medic replied, her voice impossibly calm, in the circumstances. "But he's just come out of an impossibly deep trance-like state. He's walked the void, seen the face of death and returned. I'm guessing he's massively disinhibited right now."

"So what happens now? Is there some sort of medication you can give him for that?"

Zyara shook her head. "I'm afraid we're in uncharted territory here, Sera. I've never treated anyone with this condition before. I've only read about it in medical journals."

"I am the only one who can restrain him." Tarak moved forward, but Sera stepped in his path.

"Move, female," he ordered, looming over her. "You will not be able to handle him when he's like this."

Sera shook her head, refusing to budge. She'd had a glimpse of what went on inside Xal's head back on *Ristval V*. If he was in a state where all his barriers were down, the last thing he needed was a fight.

It was instinct, more than anything else, that told her Xal needed her right now.

It just felt like the right thing to do.

"I've got this one, General," she said, meeting his crimson glare. "Please let me do this my way."

"In this state, he will hurt you."

Sera held up a hand. "The one thing I know for sure is that Xal would never hurt me." She turned and approached the door. "So I'm going to go in now, and none of you guys are going to interrupt us. That includes you." She shot the peacekeepers a harsh glare. They stared at her as if she was batshit crazy.

"Miss Aquinas, the Kordolian is dangerous. If anything happens to you, your father will—"

"So don't let him hear about it," she growled. "And turn down the heating in there. I might be a while, and I don't want to swelter to death."

Everyone was staring at her as if she'd grown a second head. Except for Tarak, who somehow managed to look resigned. "Are you sure about this, female?"

"Do I look unsure?"

He shrugged. "If you get into trouble, just scream."

"There will be no screaming, General," she said silkily, as the door slid open. "Trust me. We will be fine."

HE BECAME aware of the sound of his own heartbeat thundering in his ears. It was unbearably warm in the room, and his horns hurt like hell. They'd been cut off.

Why?

He was dimly aware of having wandered out into the brightly lit corridor, where he'd encountered the Humans. They'd tried to restrain him. He'd fought until the Kordolian medic had come and led him back to his room.

Her name escaped him right now.

Humans and Kordolians. What were they doing together?

Reality hovered at the edge of his consciousness, just out of reach. Deep down, he knew what had happened to him, but right now, he just couldn't access those memories. They were elusive and distant.

Where was he? He recalled the sensation of weightlessness and cold that was so bitter it bothered even him, a Kordolian, seeping into his bones. He remembered being suspended in nothingness and staring into warm, brown eyes through layers of glass. Those eyes had been incredibly sad.

For me? Why?

The chill was gone now, replaced with uncomfortable warmth that made his limbs sluggish and heavy. His mind contained an impenetrable fog.

He tried to latch on to the memory of that familiar brown gaze, but he felt himself slipping away, back into the void.

The void held blissful silence and enticed him with the thought of death.

The brown eyes in his mind turned into amber ones, so similar to his own. But they were blank and unfocused; sightless.

She'd been born blind.

My child.

A sensation of tightness gripped him, taking hold of his heart. The feeling grew, spreading into his limbs. Strange emotions coursed through him. Part of him wanted to lie down and close his eyes and escape back into that place of nothingness. It was so tempting.

Another part of him wanted to fight. He would fight anything and anyone.

He didn't know which parts were real anymore.

The door opened.

And there stood a Human.

I know her. That was all he knew. She stepped forward, allowing the doors behind her to close.

What's her name?

She frowned at him, putting her hands on her hips. She wore a simple grey garment that hid the sinful curves of her body, but he could still make out the swell of her breasts and the fullness of her hips.

She was completely, utterly Human; so different to him, yet so intriguing.

"Xalikian." She knew his name. It dropped from her full

lips like a sensual bomb, each syllable caressed and shaped by her exotic Human accent. "What the hell are you doing?"

She walked towards him with slow, purposeful steps, capturing his gaze with her depthless brown eyes.

"I..." His mouth opened but no words came out. He watched her move, her hips swaying with each step, mesmerizing him with their slow rhythm.

Her pink lips were slightly parted and a trace of moisture glistened on them. A faint pink hue had spread across her cheeks and her dark hair cascaded around her face, gracing her features like a wild crown.

He had never seen a creature more beautiful and more tempting than her.

"Why are you cracking skulls and breaking bones, Xal? You should know that Humans are no match for Kordolians in strength or speed. You should pick on someone your own size."

She reached him and looked up, her eyes roaming over his face, drinking him in. The way she looked at him was intense and searching and he got the feeling this look was reserved only for him.

His arousal flared to life.

His cock was impossibly hard.

He inhaled her scent. She smelled of clean linen and soap and *woman*. He was overcome with need. He wanted to taste her.

"Hey." She tilted her chin slightly, and there was a stubborn edge to her expression. "What's that look for? Why are you staring at me as if you've never seen a Human before?"

Her directness tugged at the fabric of his memories, demanding his attention.

The raw surfaces of his severed horns throbbed with an exquisite sensation; pain mixed with pleasurable anticipation.

The points of her nipples were taut and visible under the thin fabric of her garment.

It was hot in the room, and a fine sheen of moisture had appeared on her skin, making it luminous and shiny.

"You look lost," she said softly, reaching out to touch his face. She ran a thumb down the tracks of dried blood that had seeped from his cut horns. "Let me remind you of everything that exists between us."

I know you.

The memories were there; he just needed to find them. All he knew was that he wanted this female. He wanted her with every fiber in his being, and nothing would stand in his way. Through the thick fog that clouded his mind, one thought came to him.

You are mine.

"Let me see you," he rasped, his voice hoarse, as if he were using it for the first time.

"Oh, you need a little something to help jog your memory?" Her low voice was full of confidence. She understood very well the power she had over him.

He urged her with his glance, and she stepped back, pulling her drab top over her head. Underneath, her light brown skin glistened. He admired the fullness of her breasts and the rounded shape of her nipples, which he was dying to take into his mouth. The vibrantly colored artwork on her left arm came to life, highlighted by the shimmer of moisture on her skin. Vines and leaves and flowers twisted and coalesced into a network of scars that trailed up the side of her face.

She was the most beautiful thing he'd ever seen.

She tucked a thumb into the waistband of her pants and slid them over her hips, letting them drop to the floor.

His heart thudded a little louder and a little faster. His breath caught. His cock strained.

His gaze was drawn to the delicate organ between her legs. The scent of her arousal hooked into him and reeled him in and he moved towards her, a soft growl rumbling through him.

He took her chin into his hand and looked into her molten

eyes. He bent down and tasted her lips, feeling the heat of her mouth against his. Her sweetness drove him to explore her mouth, their tongues meeting as he kissed her.

He kissed her slowly, savoring every last moment. He pressed his body against hers, making her aware of his erection. She responded with a low moan, caressing him through the thin fabric of his trousers.

Her touch drove him wild. And slowly, the fog surrounding his memories started to dissipate.

"Remember me now, Xal?" Her small, mischievous smile was another hook in his heart, reeling him in.

The coldness of the void had been burnt away by her heat. He ran his hands down her neck and her shoulders, his fingers coming to her breasts. He traced over both nipples and they hardened even further, ripples of gooseflesh appearing on her skin.

Her body responded so nicely to his touch. "I'm starting to remember," he rumbled.

"Good." She reached up to touch his face, her fingers tracing upwards, grazing over his severed horns. He froze, the strangest feeling of mixed pain and pleasure spreading through his skull. They had long since stopped bleeding and the cut surface had dried, becoming hard and black.

"I loved these," she said mournfully.

"They aren't sealed," he reassured her. "They will grow back."

Her touch was driving him crazy. Her closeness was pushing him to the edge of control. His need for her was almost painful.

How was it possible that there existed a being so perfect for him?

He planted his lips on her neck, tasting salt on her skin. He trailed slow, sucking kisses down her body, claiming every inch of her.

This is all mine.

He dropped slowly to his knees and contemplated the lush mound of her sex.

Mine.

He slid his finger between the moist lips of her pussy. She whimpered. She was wonderfully, deliciously wet.

He explored her entrance, tracing his fingers over her sweet, sensitive flesh. She was so soft; so ready for him.

She threaded her fingers through his hair, expressing her enjoyment with a low, throaty moan. She quivered against him and he inserted another finger into her, going deep, making her gasp.

He applied gentle pressure against her tightness, stretching her slowly as she pressed her fingers into his skull, massaging his head, a satisfying tension transmitted through her fingertips. With her thumbs, she caressed the severed stumps of his horns, and he found himself awash with pleasure and pain.

Oh yes, she was most definitely his.

He withdrew his fingers slowly, eliciting a low growl from her. Then, he pressed his lips against her salty sweetness, savoring her taste as he slipped his long tongue between her silky folds.

He looked up and saw her exhaling, her eyes closed, her lips parted, a wonderful expression of pleasure on her face.

He moved his tongue in and out. Her face twisted, her body writhed, and she trembled. When she moaned, it was music to his ears.

He brushed his tongue against her clit and she gasped, so he did it again. And again.

The way his female responded pleased him. He watched her closely as he sucked her clit, monitoring every gasp, every sigh, every little nuance. He flicked his tongue back and forth, adjusting the speed and pressure of his caresses according to the sound of her voice, as if he were playing an instrument.

And how lovely she sounded.

Her cries were becoming louder now. Her skin was slick with moisture and her intense heat seeped into him, making him go just a little bit faster. She clutched him tighter and he trailed his fingers up her muscular thighs, reaching the fine curves of her ass.

She was helpless before him, and he would make her scream.

He went faster yet again, until she was trembling. Then, he drew back, bit by bit, making the strokes of his tongue gentler and slower, extracting every single drop of pleasure from her sweet bud.

And just when he knew she could take no more, he sucked her again.

She screamed.

He smiled.

CHAPTER TWENTY

"Sera," Xal rumbled, rising from his kneeling position. A dangerous smile played across his lips, and his wolfish eyes roamed over her possessively.

"Oh, so now you remember?" She was breathless and her legs felt like jelly. He wrapped his arms around her waist.

"Perhaps." He pressed his body against her and once again, she felt his massive erection. "However, I may need another reminder."

"There's a problem," she said, her expression turning mock-serious.

"What?" Genuine concern entered his eyes, making her laugh.

"You have far too many clothes on, Prince."

"That can be fixed," he growled, tearing off his thin black undershirt. Sera couldn't help herself. She reached out and touched his magnificent chest, trailing her fingers down his taut abdomen, where each muscle was clearly defined.

Relief flooded through her. Her impossible Prince was back from the dead, and he was very much alive.

Gone was the terrible coldness that had seeped through

his body. She traced her fingers over his smooth, silver skin and felt only warmth.

"Don't ever do that again," she murmured, as she undid his trousers.

"I won't if you won't," he replied. "No more life-threatening situations for you, my Queen."

"Same goes for you." Sera curled her arms around him, putting her head against his chest. His heart beat steadily, in time with her own. "But thank you, Xal. For saving my life."

"There was no alternative." His voice was hoarse with desire. "My existence would have been pointless if I'd left you back there."

He always managed to say these damn things that made her go weak at the knees.

"I can't hold back any longer," he growled, and Sera squealed as he scooped her into his powerful arms and brought her to a rumpled bed in the corner of the room. He lay her down and drank her in with his hungry gaze.

He moved over her, pushing her hair back from her face with a gentle hand. His eyes spoke to her of distant, mysterious worlds, and she allowed her gaze to roam over his features. Even with dried streaks of black smudged across his temples and his horns cut, he was still perfection.

The sharp, elegant lines of his features could make him appear coldly aristocratic and even cruel at times, but when he was with her, his face softened and his expression became warm. Right now, however, he was looking at her with barely restrained heat.

"I need you," he whispered, in between kisses. With one hand, he parted the lips of her pussy, which still throbbed with lingering pleasure.

"Same here." Sera drew him towards her, wrapping her legs around her back.

At first, he teased her with his mischievous finger, dipping into her wetness and growling in approval. Sera pulled him down into a slow, lingering kiss.

Gently, he withdrew his finger and entered her, his cock stretching her and filling her, and she moaned as pleasure spread through her core.

Xal began to fuck her, slowly at first, seeming to savor the moment. His mouth was on hers, warm and insistent. Sera lost all awareness of time and space as she surrendered herself to him, closing her eyes and letting him take her slow and deep.

Their bodies moved together. Xal's heat radiated into her, making sweat bead on her bare skin. His warmth surrounded her with a sensual cocoon. She inhaled his crisp, masculine scent and ran her hands over the taut ridges of muscle across his back.

This big, powerful Kordolian male was all hers, and she was going to enjoy every last inch of his body.

The intensity of their lovemaking grew as Xal thrust his powerful hips, his cock gliding against her sensitive flesh, its ridged surface brushing her clit. Her nerve-endings were stretched taut. Everything was hyper-real. She closed her eyes and saw stars in her vision. Their breathing was rough and raw, their moans and grunts of pleasure combining in a primal harmony. Every touch, every thrust and every movement edged her closer towards another climax.

Xal ran his strong fingers through her hair, making fists as he slammed against her, no longer gentle, moving faster and faster until they were both crying out, on the verge of release.

He slammed into her one last time, plunging deep.

He cried her name as he came inside her, pulling her against him, bringing her into a tight embrace as Sera was over-whelmed by another orgasm.

Afterwards, he held her as if he would never, ever let her go.

They stayed like that for a while, basking in the afterglow

of their lovemaking. They lay in companionable silence as the rate of their breathing slowed and their bodies cooled.

"I remember everything now," Xal said eventually. He sounded slightly amused. Sera looked up and saw a cheeky smile gracing his lips.

"Oh you remember now, do you?" She arched an eyebrow, tracing the remnants of his horns. He shuddered. "Was that all it took to cure you?"

"Evidently."

Sera untangled herself from him and rolled onto her side. Xal did the same, and they lay facing each other. "What happened when you did this *anava* thing, Xal? Where did you go?"

He was silent for a moment, his expression becoming thoughtful. "I don't really know. Superstitious Kordolians talk of something called the void, a place between life and death. Perhaps I was there."

Sera shuddered. "I'm glad you're back."

"As am I."

"But there's something that's been bothering me ever since we escaped from the *Ristval V*."

"I know. You saw the real me," he said grimly. "Back there, with Alerak, you saw my true nature. I'm a Kordolian, Sera, and there are certain things that will never change. From time to time, I might give in to my baser instincts. In truth, I'm no better than the Kordolians I fight against."

"Idiot." She reached over and punched him lightly. "Do you think I'd be head-over-heels for you if you were some deluded psychopath? Trust me, I know what bad people look like. I grew up in a nest of vipers. You're not one of them."

He gave her a wry look. "I suppose I have no choice but to trust your judgement on this one, Sera."

Sera took a deep breath, brushing a stray strand of hair away from Xal's face. Her next question had been on her mind for a while, and she'd debated for a long time whether to even ask it.

But she had to know. It was now or never, because the moment was slipping away.

"You said there was a child." She paused, watching Xal's face closely. "Yours."

He took a deep breath and closed his eyes. "There was a child," he admitted, his voice becoming distant. "It's funny you mention it. When I was coming out of the *anava*, I kept seeing her eyes."

"Her?"

"The only female child to be born on Kythia in this generation. My daughter. At first, they said it was a miracle."

"Oh," Sera gasped. She was quiet for a moment, as the significance of that statement sank in. "And the mother? Was she someone you loved too?"

"I never knew her mother," Xal said bitterly. "After my father died, my mother decided she wanted another heir, even though she was beyond childbearing age. She wanted a child she could shape in her own image, since I was apparently damaged goods."

"Damaged goods my ass," Sera growled. She would fight anyone who talked dirty about her Prince.

Xal smiled sadly, brushing a finger across her lips to silence her. "They held me down and extracted my seed. At first I didn't care what they did with it, but many cycles later, rumors started circulating that a child had been born. I could no longer be so indifferent."

Sera brought her arms around Xal as a tear slipped down her cheek.

"I demanded to see my child, so they brought me to her. I watched her from behind sterile glass and something shifted inside me. This was my child, Sera. Mine. I was a fool for thinking I could sit back while my mother took her away from me."

Sera looked into his golden eyes and saw a world of pain and regret. She pulled him closer.

"They wouldn't allow me to touch her. When I tried to take her away, the Imperial Guard intervened on the orders of the Empress. There was nothing I could do."

"That's awful."

"That's Kythia, Sera. Kordolians play with life and death as if they are gods. Of course, I couldn't accept that. I began to plot to take her from my mother, but it was too late. As she grew, they had noticed that something was wrong. Her eyes, the exact same shade as my own, didn't see. She was blind." Xal's voice was hollow and empty.

Dread wormed its way into Sera's chest. "But that shouldn't be a problem."

"My mother saw it differently. You see, a prophet had once told her that the end of the Empire would be brought about by the birth of a sightless daughter. For some reason, she became obsessed with that foretelling. So when they found out my daughter was blind, they had her killed. All because of some stupid prophecy. My child, Sera. They killed my child. I never thought they could sink that low. I should have figured it out sooner." Xal was still in her arms. "I don't believe in prophecy, but perhaps this foretelling is coming true as we speak. When I found out my child's life was no more, I was overcome with grief and rage. I picked up a dagger and went and stabbed the Empress in the heart. She was extremely lucky to survive. So you see, I am equally as monstrous as her." Xal's face was chillingly serene, but his voice cracked a little. "They hadn't even named her yet. I hadn't named my daughter."

Silence stretched between them, and for a while, Sera couldn't speak.

Tears were streaming down her face. Xal kissed her cheek and wiped the wetness from her eyes. "What's this?"

"I never cry, Xal. On Earth I have a reputation for being a hard-ass. But I'm just—" She sniffed.

"You're sad."

"Don't Kordolians cry when they're sad?"

"Crying must be a Human trait. For us, there is no way to express sadness. Some Kordolians refuse to believe things such emotions even exist."

"That's bullshit. You're allowed to be sad, Xal. You're allowed to show it, too." She sniffed loudly. "I'm so sorry."

"Whatever for?" He kissed her again, tasting her salty tears. "The past cannot be changed, and none of it was your fault. But thank you, Sera, for being sad for me. I don't deserve it."

"You deserve it, Xal, and so does that poor little one." Sera closed her eyes and Xal held her tightly in his arms, kissing her softly on the top of her head. She drifted off to the soothing sound of his steadily beating heart. Thoughts of dark, distant planets and cruel Empires entered her mind as Xal's warmth surrounded her, and she suddenly yearned for the bright, warm sunshine of Earth.

She couldn't wait to go back, and Xal was coming with her. What he had told her shocked her to the core, but she understood now that he would do anything to protect her. He would never hurt her. There were worse things she could think of than being overrun by a bunch of fierce, protective Kordolians. Her people would just have to accept the fact that the Kordolians were here to stay.

Humans would get used to the idea, one way or another.

———

XAL LOOKED up as the doors to the tiny room slid open. Sera lay in his arms, asleep.

"What do you want?" He glared at the Human soldiers crowding the doorway, their weapons raised at him. They flinched at the sound of his voice.

He had vague memories of fighting Humans in the corridor.

One of the men spoke, his eyes growing wide as he glanced at Sera. "Uh, Senator Aquinas is on the comm. He's demanding to speak with his daughter."

The Humans were staring. Xal pulled the blanket up, covering Sera's shoulders. "Lower your voice, soldier," he said softly. "Can't you see that she's sleeping? Tell him to check back later, when she's awake."

"We can't leave the Senator waiting. He's a very important—"

"I don't care if he's the fucking Emperor of Earth. Get. Out." Xal bared his fangs and the soldiers froze, wary of him. They had guns, but they wouldn't use them with Sera in the room.

The man who had spoken before sighed. "Look man, we'd rather not wake her either, but her old man's got a short fuse. The three of us could be out of a job if we go back without her."

Sera stirred, opening her eyes slowly. "Xal? What's going on?" She looked up and saw the Human soldiers. "Is there a problem?"

"Miss Aquinas, there's a call from your father." The soldier looked extremely relieved that she was awake. "He wants to speak with you right now."

Sera stretched languidly. She didn't seem to care that three Human males were staring at her barely concealed body. Xal growled.

Under the covers, she placed a reassuring hand on his chest. "Give us a minute, guys. I'll be right out."

Xal glared at the Humans as they disappeared.

Sera rolled her eyes. "I'll handle this. Dad can get a bit cranky sometimes. I don't want those poor boys to lose their jobs." She gave him a long, slow-burning kiss before she slid out of bed and picked her clothes off the floor. Xal watched her as she started to dress, admiring her toned body.

"He's probably going nuts wondering why both Kordolian warships have suddenly left Earth's orbit. See, he's vying for the post of Galactic Affairs Minister, which is currently vacant. He likes to be kept in the loop on such things. I bet all of Earth has been going crazy since we left."

Xal shrugged. "You will tell them the truth about us."

"I think I've compiled enough convincing evidence that you guys aren't going to take over Earth and ship us all off to the mines, but I'm not going to tell them the whole truth." She winked. "Some things have to be left to the imagination."

Suddenly, Sera was straddling him, her strong, rough hands holding him down. "You're coming with me, right?"

Xal gripped her wrists, bringing her hands up to his severed horns. She ran her thumbs over them, making him shudder. As their surface healed, laying down new tissue, they felt less painful and more sensitive. He was becoming aroused again. "I believe the opposite is true. As my mate, you are coming to Earth with me."

"Mate?" A sexy smile curved her lips.

"Any objections, Sera?"

"None, my Prince."

"Good." His lips quirked. "But you had better stop calling me by that title, because I am no longer of the Empire. I've relinquished all ties. From now on, I'm just a simple, humble, ordinary Kordolian."

Sera laughed. "Yeah, right. Simple and humble my ass. I'll call you Prince when it suits me, because we Humans seem to be awfully impressed by that sort of stuff. Trust me. You'll get much more done on Earth if you throw your weight around a bit and act Imperial now and then. So don't abandon the title just yet."

"I'll keep that in mind for when I'm dealing with Humans like your father."

"Exactly." He loved it when she smiled mischievously like that. "I can't wait to introduce you to him."

"I get the feeling your advice on managing Humans will be invaluable when it comes to diplomatic matters."

"You overestimate me," she said innocently. "I'm just a humble journalist who happened to grow up in the belly of the beast."

"There's nothing humble about you, my Queen."

She proved his point by walking out of the room with her head held high, her hips swaying suggestively, making him hard all over again.

CHAPTER TWENTY-ONE

"Sera, what the hell do you think you're doing, bringing those aliens onboard a key company asset? When I told you to go and negotiate with Prince Xalikian, I didn't mean for you to go into space and invite them onto the *MS Elvis*. Are you out of your mind? Sometimes I think that accident left you permanently brain-damaged."

Sera leaned back in the swivel chair, putting her slipper-clad feet on the table as she stared at the projected image of her father. Senator Julian Aquinas was in his office, leaning back in his large leather chair. Since he'd been elected, he'd seemed to age before her very eyes, his dark hair turning grey at the temples, the lines in his face deepening.

"Dad," she said, noticing the faint haze that drifted across his face. "Have you been smoking?"

He waved his hand in the air. "That's none of your business, Sera. You need to get those aliens off my mining station."

"Mom will kill you if she finds out you're smoking again."

He pointedly ignored her. "And you'd better have some news for me about what the Kordolians are really doing here. I don't like the fact that they just up and left all of a sudden. They're preparing for an invasion down here on

Earth. People are panicking. Your article started all this, Sera."

"They're not going to invade Earth." Sera smiled sweetly. "All they want to do is integrate."

"Integrate?" Her father looked at her as if she were out of her mind.

"Trust me, dad, they could do terrible things to us if they wanted to, but they haven't. I'll be putting out a new article in the next few days. I'll also give you some information so the Federation can put out an official statement. They're not here to colonize us."

"Then what the hell do they want?"

"They want to find mates. Kordolians have a particular interest in Human women."

"You can't seriously believe that."

"It's true." Sera grinned. "Believe me, it's true."

"What exactly have you been doing with those Kordolians, Sera?" Suspicion entered her father's voice. "Have they threatened you somehow? Have they done something to you? Is that why you're saying these things?"

"Senator Aquinas," Sera said softly. "What was the purpose of this communication?"

Her father froze, taken aback by her use of his formal title. "What do you mean? I'd received some urgent notifications about the *Elvis*. That my daughter had appeared out of nowhere with three Kordolians, one of whom had seriously injured several of my staff. What did you think this comm was about?"

"Oh, I don't know," Sera shrugged. "I thought you might be worried about me or something."

"Sera," her father sighed, running a hand through his greying hair. "I learnt to stop worrying about you when you left home. Otherwise, I think I'd have died of stress by now. You're always going to do what you want, and nobody's going to stop you. That was obvious even when you were a child."

"If I'm as stubborn as you say, what makes you think I would be so easily influenced by these Kordolians?"

The Senator blinked. Sera smirked. He wasn't used to being contradicted.

"You have a point," he said reluctantly. "But we can't afford to let our guard down."

"Dad, you know I'm always skeptical until proven otherwise. And what I've seen leads me to believe these guys aren't so bad. Besides, whether we like it or not, they aren't going away."

"And what about the threat to Earth?"

"Let's just say Kordolian politics is a little complicated. They're not all on the same side. The last I heard, our Kordolians were chasing off the threat. I'll keep you posted on how that goes."

"*Our* Kordolians?" Her father raised an eyebrow.

Sera smiled cryptically. "They're here to make love, not war."

The senator dropped his face into his hand, rubbing his eyes. "You're a problem child, Sera. Just get them off my facility. I don't want to have to explain to the Senate that Kordolians were spotted boarding one of my assets. I can't afford any scandals right now, Sera."

"Yes, Sir." Sera raised her hand in a mock-salute. Her father gave her a funny look, as if he didn't quite trust her. He was right, of course. When the Earthlings found out that Xal and Sera were an item, there was going to be scandal; lots of it.

Not that Sera gave a shit. Besides, she now had a fierce Kordolian warrior at her side to help scare off the paparazzi.

She couldn't wait to get back to Earth. They were going to have so much fun.

ONE OF THE injured soldiers yelled loudly in some Earth

language as Xal appeared in the doorway. It was a cry for help. He jumped out of the bunk, grabbing some sort of metal apparatus on wheels and brandishing it in front of him as Xal approached.

Xal held up his hands in what he hoped was a placating gesture. "I'm not going to hurt you, Human," he said in Universal.

"G-get out of here, Kordolian! The peacekeepers are on their way."

"Relax," Xal said, a little too forcefully. "I came here to apologize."

"Apologize?" The soldier held up his arm. It was bound in some sort of solid support. "You broke my fucking arm, man. And they don't have the facilities to do rapid bone regen here, so I'm stuck in a cast for the next six weeks."

Vague memories of smashing this man against the wall entered Xal's mind.

The soldier winced. "And you've cracked three of my ribs. It hurts like hell, man."

"Hey, Johnson, take it easy." Another soldier sat in the corner with his leg bound and elevated. "If he was going to whoop your ass he would have done so already, isn't that right, Kordolian?"

Xal acknowledged the man by inclining his head. "The Human is correct."

Footsteps sounded from outside, and a group of armed guards appeared. "Freeze!"

Xal took a step back, holding up his hands. "Easy, I only wanted to talk."

The leader of this particular squad was a green-eyed female with dark, braided hair. She pointed her weapon at him. "How did you get down here, Kordolian? This is a secure area. You need to get back to your quarters." Her voice was flat and emotionless. If she was uneasy, she didn't let it show, unlike the hothead with the injured arm.

Xal shifted so that he could see all of the Humans. "I understand if my presence makes you feel uncomfortable, but please, hear me out." He focused on the injured Humans. "I'm aware that I may have been a little, uh, rough on you. Please accept my most sincere apologies for any injuries I've caused you. I was not in a good way back there. I can assure you I mean no you no harm whatsoever." Xal figured that if Humans and Kordolians were to live side-by-side, there had to be some sort of mutual understanding.

Humans were naturally afraid of his kind. He didn't blame them. The ever-present threat of invasion was very real.

Coming out of *anava*, he'd hurt these soldiers. He didn't want that to become a sore point with the Humans, so he'd decided he had to make things right.

The guy with the broken arm snorted. "Says the guy who put three of us in the infirmary."

Xal fought to keep his expression calm and non-threatening, but the Human's refusal to accept his apology was starting to irritate him. "Again," he grated, "I apologize. I'll make a point of mentioning your dedication and commitment to Sera's father when I meet him."

The Humans traded strange looks. "You're going to meet the Big Cheese? I don't think you understand how it works on Earth, Kordolian." The man with the broken leg wore a cynical expression. "You see, our corporations are a bit like brothels. You need special introductions to get inside, and even then, the madam of the house will only pay attention to you if you have lots and lots of money. The Aquinas girl's old man is like the madam, only he also runs the legit coffee-shop on the surface and the department store across the road. So I appreciate the sentiment and all, but you probably won't end up scoring a meeting with him that easily."

Xal had no idea what the man was talking about. He wondered if he was a bit delirious from the pain medication. Humans seemed to babble a lot, and they said some strange things at times. "If the father of my mate ever considers himself too busy to meet me, he's going to have problems," he said mildly. "Let us hope that isn't the case."

"Mate?" Several of the Humans blurted the word at the same time. The human with the broken leg gaped.

"As in, you and the Big Cheese's daughter are—"

"Is there a problem?" Xal's voice became low and dangerous. He wouldn't have them saying anything bad about their relationship.

The Humans stared blankly at him.

"No? Well in that case, I extend greetings to you from the New Kordolian State. I look forward to a mutually beneficial relationship between our people." Xal smiled, baring his fangs. "Believe me, we are now very much in your corner, so you have nothing to worry about."

CHAPTER TWENTY-TWO

Sera couldn't believe it. They were being held up at the immigration station because she had forgotten to renew her Universal passport.

"Sorry, Miss Aquinas. You're going to have to fill in a Temporary Entry form and pay a fee of five hundred credits. Your retinal scan checks out, but it's showing that your passport is expired." The immigration officer handed her a data port.

Beside her, Xal watched with a look of mild exasperation. The immigration officer's gaze kept drifting to him. Ever since they'd docked and entered the station, they'd been attracting stares from the various aliens and Humans entering Earth.

That's what happened when you had two big, intimidating Kordolians on either side of you.

The General stood behind them, impatience radiating from every pore. The longer he was away from Abbey, the more irritable he became. Sera was starting to worry that he might seriously hurt someone.

"Uh, sorry guys," she said sheepishly. "I haven't been off-planet for a long time. I guess I'd forgotten about my passport."

She synced some data from her link-bracelet and handed

the data port back to the officer. "That's been paid. How long will it take to process my entry?"

"You should be cleared in, hang on," he peered at his holoscreen as the data transferred. "Done. You're good to go, ma'am." The officer cleared his throat nervously. Xal and Tarak pinned the poor guy with their intense stares.

"Um, as for the Kordolians," he said thinly, referring to the elephant in the room, "they're going to have to get ambassadorial clearance."

"Enough," growled Tarak. "Why do Humans insist on following such convoluted procedures? I did not risk my soldiers and defeat an Imperial warship just so I could return to Earth to be herded around like some pathetic *vorchek.*" He glared at the official, who was glancing towards the peacekeepers stationed to one side of the hall. "My mate is on Earth. I need to go to her. Why must you make it so complicated?"

"Tarak," Xal shot him a meaningful glare. "We agreed to abide by Human customs, and this 'bureaucracy', as they call it, is one of them. If we are to engage with the Humans, it needs to be on their terms. Or at least, they must think that it's on their terms. I'm sure Abbey would agree."

Tarak remained silent. The air suddenly felt very oppressive. Sera squeezed Xal's hand.

Xal sighed. "I know what you're thinking. It would be easier just to forcibly enter Earth. But then we wouldn't be any better than the Imperial forces. I'm trying to cultivate an image here, General."

"Humans are freaking out right now," Sera added. "If they see a big, black, scary looking thing in the sky, they'll think an invasion is happening."

"Do you think I care whether the Humans 'freak out' or not? They can do what they like. I just want to get back to Abbey."

The wide-eyed official stepped away from his desk. "Um,

I'll just go and get the Prime Ambassador," he stuttered, before disappearing behind a door.

Tarak shot Xal and Sera a dark look. "This is all your fault, Prince. You insisted on abiding by these ridiculous Human rules."

Xal shrugged. "As I said, it's all about image. I want to develop a reputation for being friendly."

The General stared at him as if he were out of his mind.

The immigration officer returned with a man in a dark suit, who took one look at Xal and Tarak and sighed. "You've returned, Prince," he said. "Why don't you all come to my office, so we can talk?"

Tarak glowered. Xal smiled. Sera remained quiet, looking at both Kordolian males, who towered over her. Xal appeared relaxed. Tarak was seething with impatience.

"Do you require an escort?" The officer regarded the Kordolians with trepidation. "I'll call for some peacekeepers."

"Not necessary." The Ambassador said, with a dismissive wave of his hand. "If they wanted to harm us we'd be dead already, am I right, Prince?"

Xal said nothing, responding with an innocent shrug. They followed the Ambassador down a network of back corridors. He led them past a discreet reception area that was decorated with a vase of fresh lilies. Their unique perfume filled the air. It was such an odd extravagance to have on an orbiting immigration station; a reminder of the life that existed below on planet Earth.

As they sat, the Ambassador stroked his white beard, the only indication that he might be uneasy. "I'll get straight to the point," he said. "The Federation is completely mystified by recent events. What we know is that there were two Kordolian warships orbiting Earth. Both of them disappeared, and only one returned. Your actions are causing dissent amongst the citizens on Earth. I have spoken to Senator Aquinas and President Jiao. We request that you attend a special Senate Hearing to discuss the terms of a potential Human-Kordolian alliance."

Xal smiled, his fangs gleaming. Sera knew he was trying to appear friendly, but he still had the aura of a predator about him. That was how Kordolians were. Tall, silver, pointy-eared and dangerous. There was only so much they could tame their true nature, and Sera wouldn't have it any other way.

"That sounds perfect, Ambassador Rahman," he said. "We will lay this matter to rest once and for all." He turned to Sera with glowing pride in his eyes. "My mate has chronicled everything and her actions have saved your planet a great deal of trouble. You have no idea of what she has gone through to save your people."

The Ambassador's eyes widened. He looked at Sera with growing alarm. "You're Julian's daughter, aren't you?"

"So what if I am?" Sera crossed her arms, preparing to get defensive. But to her surprise, Ambassador Rahman grinned.

"It will be good to see the old man out of his depth for once. He's gotten far too comfortable these past few years. It's good to shake things up now and then, wouldn't you agree?"

Tarak glowered impatiently. Xal and Sera smiled. Through the high window, they could see the outline of Earth. It was in shadow, etched with glittering networks of golden lights.

"Welcome back to Earth," Ambassador Rahman said ironically, with a quirk of his eyebrow. "I do hope you will enjoy all that we have to offer."

CHAPTER TWENTY-THREE

Sera stood in the corner of the giant ballroom, sipping her whiskey and watching the crowd. The who's who of international politics were congregated in this room, dressed in black-tie finery. Aliens mingled with the Humans, most clad in their traditional formal attire.

A congregation of Avein delegates stood close to her, sampling the buffet and looking quite ethereal with their large black wings. She saw a group of aliens she didn't recognize; these guys had black scales and four arms. They wore striking, deep red robes.

"I'm surprised to see you here, sister."

Sera turned. Her older sister Avery stood behind her. Avery was statuesque and slender, her artificially straightened hair dyed blonde and arranged in an elaborate updo. She wore a shimmering lilac gown and and a glittering diamond necklace that probably cost as much as a small island in the Pacific.

She looked Sera up and down with a hint of disapproval in her eyes. Sera wore all white; a fitted, satin tuxedo jacket and slim white trousers that hugged her toned legs. Her curly hair was tamed into a quiff and her face was free of any make-up. A pair of glittering onyx chandelier earrings were her only adornment.

Avery smiled, but there was no warmth in her eyes. "We haven't seen you in a long time, dear sister. To be honest, I didn't think you would show up, since you're so busy with that little job of yours."

"Wait until Monday," Sera said mildly. That's when she'd scheduled the release of her latest story, along with carefully edited footage from her time onboard *Silence*. "Then you'll see what I've been doing in my 'job'."

"Maybe," Avery smirked. "But I'm a bit too busy to go over every minor news story that comes out. I've got my final law exams in two weeks. Once I graduate, it's straight to the company boardroom. It's a shame you didn't choose to work for the family, Sera. You could have gone far by now."

"Apparently, I didn't fit the psychometric profile," Sera said nonchalantly. "And I'm quite happy with my job, Avery." Sera sipped her drink as a man came up behind Avery, greeting her with a peck on the cheek. This guy looked about ten years younger than her sister. He flashed his teeth in a too-perfect white smile.

"George, meet Sera," Avery said smugly. "She's the sister I told you about."

"Oh, so you're the one?" George held out a manicured hand, greeting her with a raised eyebrow and an empty "nice to meet you." Sera shook it with the grip of a seasoned fighter, making him wince. She knew his type. Every time they met, which was admittedly rarely, Avery had a different young pretty-boy hanging off her arm.

George must be her latest acquisition.

"You haven't brought a date, Sera?" Avery asked pointedly. Sera's perpetual single status had long been a source of speculation amongst the family.

"I'm expecting someone," Sera replied, sipping her

whiskey in a relaxed manner. Avery raised a skeptical eyebrow.

"You had better be," a familiar low voice rumbled behind her. The next thing she knew, a possessive hand was on her waist, and Sera was being pulled into a kiss. Xal's lips were warm and insistent, and he kissed her unashamedly.

"You look stunning, Sera," he rumbled, as Avery and George stared at them in shock.

Enjoying her sister's discomfort, Sera took a moment to check Xal out. He'd taken her advice and gone for the regal prince look, this time wearing a tailored black jacket with silver trimmings. It accentuated his broad shoulders and narrow waist. His horns had already started to grow back, forming small points at his temples. He'd left his beautiful white hair loose, adding a touch of wildness to his refined appearance.

Sera watched Avery's blue eyes go wide. Her sister struggled to regain her composure. It was all quite hilarious. "Meet my date," she said, twining her fingers with Xal's.

Xal held out his other hand in a perfectly executed handshake. He'd obviously been practicing his Human manners. "Xalikian Kazharan." He shook both Avery and George's hands in turn.

"And who might these Humans be, my love?" He managed sound imperial and disdainful, but his eyes sparkled with mischief as he looked at her.

"Xal, meet my sister, Avery, and, uh, George."

Xal nodded as the Humans stared at him, unable to disguise their fascination. "You're one of those guys," George blurted. "Shit, we thought we were all screwed when you showed up in Earth's orbit. You don't know how many sleepless nights I've had worrying about the invasion, man."

Beside him, Avery managed to look infuriated. Inwardly, Sera smiled. He was just a kid, after all; it became obvious when he opened his mouth. He probably wasn't even out of college yet.

Xal's expression turned deadpan. "We considered that option," he said seriously, "but I think Sera would be mad at me if I did something like that. An alliance will suffice, for now." He said the last part rather ominously.

George paled and Avery looked dazed. Sera started to pull Xal away. "Well, it's been nice catching up, dear sister and George. Perhaps I'll see you again in a year's time at the next Ambassador's Ball."

Xal nodded as Sera dragged him away. She led him out onto a balcony overlooking the sea. Thankfully, everyone else was inside, leaving them alone with the soothing sounds of the ocean.

"I know it's fun, but don't scare the Humans too much," Sera growled, as Xal pulled her towards him.

"Sorry," Xal replied, tracing his fingers around her waist. "I just couldn't resist after I saw her looking at you that way. If she was Kordolian, she'd do quite well for herself on Kythia. But enough about her. May I just re-iterate that you look incredible, Sera Aquinas?"

"Speak for yourself." Sera snuggled against him, enjoying his warmth as they looked out towards the inky blackness of the Pacific Ocean.

"Your planet never ceases to amaze me," Xal murmured. "Look at this place. It's incredible." He stared out at the sea. Sera couldn't see a thing, but she knew Xal could make out every detail in the darkness.

Kordolians, after all, were creatures of darkness.

"I can't believe you Humans have been quietly sitting on a hidden paradise all the way out in this remote sector. Kythia is a veritable shithole compared to your lush planet, Sera."

The wind buffeted them, teasing Xal's hair and carrying a faint hint of mist and salt. "Well it's your home now, Xal. I'm glad you like it."

"Apart from your infernal sun," he grumbled. "But those sunglasses you gave me work wonders."

"So are we going to see any more evil Kordolians trying to attack Earth?"

"Not if we can help it. *Silence* chased *Ristval V* to the edge of Sector Nine, where they found a wormhole. That's how they arrived here without detection in the first place. In the end, they chose to flee rather than engage. When Daegan and Alerak tried to escape by returning to the wormhole, *Silence* fired a highly destructive fission missile after them, collapsing it. I don't think we'll be seeing them again anytime soon, if at all they survived. And if they come back, we'll be ready."

"So now it's just you guys and us."

"It's just you and me, Sera, the way I like it." He tightened his arms around her waist and she leaned into him. This had to be the best Ambassador's Ball she'd ever attended, just because Xal was here with her. She usually dreaded these kinds of functions.

For Xal, it was an invaluable opportunity to mingle with the representatives of Earth and other planets and gain some useful contacts.

"I thought at least Tarak and Abbey might join us for this occasion?"

"Goddess, no. He hates formality. This would be torture for him. Besides, he's not leaving Abbey's side for a while. Personally, I'm planning to steer clear of both of them for a while. He's become irritable and overly protective. Didn't you hear? She's with child."

"Holy moly." Sera whispered. "Then what you told me about Humans and Kordolians and our uh, biology is true."

"Did you have any reason to doubt me?" Xal pulled her closer as the sea roared below, its rhythm soothing and familiar. "After all we've been through?"

"No," Sera said. "It's just that hearing about it actually happening really hits home."

"I'm excited about the possibilities," he whispered. Sera detected pain, but also tentative hope in his voice.

"So am I," she said, and for a while they just stood there, looking out at the sea. There was so much left unspoken; so much she knew Xal would rather leave unsaid. It was all too raw for him; too painful. Silently, Sera vowed to honor the precious lives he had lost.

There was still so much she had to show him on Earth as he forged a new path for himself and his people.

The Universe was ever-changing. Nothing stood still.

But there was one thing Sera knew for certain. She had found her Kordolian Prince, and there was no way she was letting him go.

That was absolute.

CHAPTER TWENTY-FOUR

Xal stared out at the Humans who were assembled in what they called the Federation Senate. This seemed to be their equivalent of the Kordolian High Council, but based on what Sera had explained to him, positions were won through merit, lobbying, and hard work.

Well, most of the time, anyway.

This was a much better system that what existed on Kythia. On occasion, Humans could be surprisingly sensible. As a race, they were much more complicated and developed than he had initially thought.

In front of him was a small device called a microphone, which apparently amplified his voice.

Xal leaned forward. This was his chance to put the matter to rest, once and for all.

Across from him sat a man he recognized as Sera's father. The elder Aquinas sat impassively, his strangely colored blue eyes watching Xal's every move.

"There has been some confusion and misinformation of late," he began, as a sea of faces turned towards him. "I have been told that Humans are afraid. Some believe we are here to colonize Earth and become your overlords. I want to categorically state that this is not the case. You all know very well that if we wanted to do such a thing we could. Human military technology isn't advanced enough for you to defend against us."

Murmurs echoed throughout the large space as his words sank in. The Humans sounded dissatisfied. No-one liked being told that their defenses were essentially useless.

"And yet, we have done no such thing," Xal continued, demanding their attention once again. "Only recently, a hostile Kordolian warship arrived in Earth's orbit. It was sent by the Old Kordolian Empire to try and take back critical military assets we had claimed. They threatened to destroy Earth. We launched an operation that drove them off. This operation would not have been successful without the help of a certain Human. By now you have all seen the footage and read the reports of your daughter, Sera Aquinas. You know what happened. If not for her, you might not be sitting here today."

Xal cast his eyes across the room, meeting each gaze in turn. "Sera is my mate." He paused as the implications of his statement sank in. He looked at Senator Aquinas. The man's face was like stone, his jaw clenched tight. Xal returned his stare. "Should anyone or anything threaten her or the planet she lives on, we will not hesitate to fight to the death to keep her safe. General Akkadian would do the same for his mate. You are at risk, Humans. Whether it be from Zarthians, Kordolians, or Xargek, the word is out. Sooner or later, you are going to be overrun if you don't have protection. That is why I wish to propose an alliance between Humans and Kordolians. In exchange for being granted asylum on your planet, we will provide you with all our military resources. It is obvious that you need us on Earth." He looked up and saw Sera sitting in the gallery. She winked at him. Xal resisted the urge to smile indulgently at her. That wouldn't do. Not when he was addressing the leaders of Earth.

"So I will put this to you, leaders of Earth. We are here,

and we intend to stay. My question to you is: are you ready to accept us?"

He stepped away from the microphone and left the leaders of Earth to discuss their options.

Regardless of what they decided, he had made up his mind.

He wasn't going anywhere.

SERA SAT on the stone bench, enjoying the bright sunshine and sipping a latte as Xal emerged from the Senate Chambers. As he stepped out into the light, he winced and pulled out the pair of vintage Ray Bans she had bought for him. He donned a broad-brimmed hat that cast a deep shadow over his face.

The hat was also a gift from her. She'd had it modified, adding a pair of neat openings that accommodated his beautiful horns.

Kordolians were sensitive to light, some more than others. Without the hat, Xal's silver skin would probably blister and peel within a few minutes.

Sera grinned. The hat looked good on him, though. *Everything* looked good on Xal. With his long, platinum hair, dark Kordolian suit and sunglasses, he looked like some sort of alien rock star.

Excited squeals reached her ears and Sera was bemused to see a group of teenaged schoolgirls intercept Xal as he headed towards her.

They babbled excitedly amongst themselves before one of them worked up the nerve to approach Xal.

"Um, Mister, can we get a photo with you?" Unlike most older Humans, they had no problem speaking Universal.

Xal looked down at them in surprise. "A photo?"

Sera almost choked on her coffee as she tried to suppress her laughter.

"Please?" The three girls, who looked as if they were about fourteen, giggled.

"Uh, I'm not sure what this is all about, but sure." Xal stood awkwardly as the teenagers surrounded him, pouting as one of them released her drone cam. It flew into the air, clicking and snapping. The girls giggled some more, while Xal just looked confused.

Sera smirked at him as his expression turned into one of mild distress. Her suspicions were correct. Kordolians were going to be the next big thing on Earth.

Xal had already managed to attract fangirls.

She waited until they had taken a few more photos before taking pity on Xal. She swooped in to rescue him as the school-girls started asking him questions.

"So, are you guys, like, taking over Earth?" They stared at Xal with undisguised fascination, as if he were an exotic bird.

"Why does everyone keep asking me that?" Xal said mildly. "Of course we aren't."

"Do you have a girlfriend?" They were becoming bolder now. Sera ambushed them from behind.

"That's enough, kids," she snapped, waving them away. "Stop pestering the poor Kordolian."

"Sera." Xal shot her the most brilliant smile, looking slightly relieved. She melted inside all over again. Sera reached his side and he greeted her with a kiss. The schoolgirls seemed slightly disappointed.

That's right girls, Sera thought smugly, *he's all mine*.

She was feeling jealous and possessive because of some teenaged schoolgirls. Oh, this was getting out of hand.

Sera placed a reassuring hand on Xal's arm. "Those photos will be circulating across the Networks in, oh, give it about half an hour. It'll be excellent PR, so don't worry. Never underesti-mate the power of a teenage selfie."

"Let's get out of here," Xal murmured, and although she couldn't see his eyes behind the dark glasses, she knew what he was thinking, because she was thinking exactly the same thing.

"Agreed." Sera took his hand into hers. "Remind me to teach you a few things about social media, fangirls and public relations."

"The perils of life on Earth?"

"You bet. Some things never change, and this is a centuries-old phenomenon. Prepare yourself for an onslaught of the curious and the obsessed. The majority, I suspect, will be female."

"I'm not worried in the least," Xal grinned, "because I have you, my fierce Queen, to scare them off."

"You're such a dork," Sera said affectionately as they walked down the imposing steps of Federation Hill, looking out at the impossibly blue expanse of the ocean below. The sight of the water gave Sera an idea, and she regarded Xal with a sly sidelong glance. "Now that we're back, I can't wait to go skinny-dipping with you in the ocean... after sundown, of course."

"Skinny-dipping?" The corner of Xal's mouth quirked upwards in amusement. "That sounds like something interesting."

"You don't even know what skinny dipping is, do you?"

"No, but I'm willing to find out," Xal rumbled, and even though he was wearing sunglasses, she could feel the heat in his stare.

"I think you'll be pleasantly surprised."

"I look forward to the surprise, then. You and this incredible planet of yours never cease to amaze me."

The sun shone down on them as they left the Senate Chambers, leaving the leaders of the world to debate over Earth's future. They were a striking sight; a Human and a Kordolian walking side-by-side in the bright morning light. Around them, people stopped to stare, but instead of being bothered by it, all Xal did was wrap a possessive arm around Sera's waist.

Sera smiled. It was going to be another gorgeous day on Nova Terra.

Printed in Great Britain
by Amazon